Read

AZRAEL: ANGEL OF DEATH

A Novel by

C. B. Wiland

authorHOUSE®

AuthorHouse™
1663 Liberty Drive, Suite 200
Bloomington, IN 47403
www.authorhouse.com
Phone: 1-800-839-8640

First published by AuthorHouse 11/15/2007

ISBN: 978-1-4343-4747-3 (sc)
ISBN: 978-1-4343-4748-0 (hc)

Library of Congress Control Number: 2007908241

Printed in the United States of America
Bloomington, Indiana

This book is printed on acid-free paper.

Disclaimer:
This is a work of fiction. The Tampa, Florida, Police department was undergoing reorganization at the time of this writing. Therefore, the structure may differ from the one described herein. The events described are imaginary, and the names and descriptions of any character to persons living or dead is purely coincidental. The events are a product of the author's imagination, and should not be inferred to reflect an actual case.

Other Novels by Author

The Pygmy

The Survivors' Affair

Ethan's Son

The Unattended Passion

Death on Hold

The Affair of the Mayan Princess

The Misogynist (The Pygmy Revisited - 2008)

Dedication

To all who have supported my efforts with particular mention of my dear wife Barbara and good friend George Ihnat, both of whom always tell it like it is. An author's ego requires support from such as these.

Foreword

It isn't news, but I'll say it anyway: Love means different things to different people. In today's portrayals and parlance, it is typically presented in wildly--often perversely--sensual terms. It's all about sex, sex, and more sex. To one reared in a more romantic era, I miss protagonists who would defend a woman's honor with their last drop of blood. I miss heroines who were modest, chaste and loyal, who didn't bounce around on beaches, breasts bared and a bottles of beer in their mouths.

So I was and am a romantic. And if my story seems overly romantic in concept, blame it on the likes of C. S. Forester, Alexander Dumas, Lloyd C. Douglas, et.al. And, of course, I'm turned on by romantic poetry. Poe used drugs. So what. In his moments of clarity, he reached into the stars and captured intense beauty and pathos in technically amazing poems such as *Annabel Lee*. Emily Dickinson never knew a man. So what. In *Patterns,* she created a powerful statement of love and despair over the death of one.

Yes, we've come a long way since Romeo took a fatal dose of poison from Juliet's lips. Extremely romantic? Of course. But far nobler than the transient and hedonistic relationships that pass for love in today's tawdry, popular culture.

Principal Characters

Azrael: The Angel of death - One of the following characters.

(Lt.)Luis Agosto - Acting head of homicide & lead investigator of Azrael murders.

(Dr.) Agnostic (Agnes) Broadhurst - Head of Forensics Unit.

(Dr..) Milton Bosch - Medical examiner and former detective.

Pete Davidson - One of five rapists. The first to die.

Angelo Donato - Second rapist to die.

Donna (Midge) Infante - Angelo Donato's friend. The unwitting host of his murder.

Dewayne Jackson -Lead investigator of April Perry's rape, who becomes head of Major Crimes Bureau in part two.

Rich Martino- Patrolman who finds April following the rape. Paxton's first partner.

Frank Panteras - Fourth rapist to die.

Brad "Rock" Paxton - Conflicted Detective Intern who must deal with the fact that the woman he loves may be killing the youths who raped her.

Tommy Perdue - Ex-fighter employed by the Perry family as a security man.

April Perry - Innocent girl whose rape triggers a series of murders for revenge years after the fact. .

Maggie Perry - April's psychotic mother who wants the five rapists dead.

Preston Perry - Head of an international law firm. April's wealthy father.

Misha Pulaski - Third rapist to die.

Josh Sampson - Leader of the rapist gang. Last man on Azrael's list.

(Major) Beryl Tankersly - Head of Criminal Investigations Division

PART ONE

In the Beginning

Tears of sorrow don't necessarily diminish a man's stature among men. Under some conditions, however, a lack of tears could be the mark of a sociopath.

CBW '07

1

In the Beginning: It was ten years ago that I noticed April Perry for the first time. It was spring in Florida--really the best time of the year--and I was sitting on a rickety bench on the front campus of Armwood High School. FYI Armwood is a large school in suburban Tampa, Florida.

Anyway, I had just finished my lunch, a ham salad sandwich, which mom actually made from bologna. Why she called it ham salad, I'll never know. Maybe "ham" salad sounded more elegant than "bologna" salad. Doesn't really matter. I liked her "ham" sandwiches then. Still do.

Back to my story. Sorry for the diversion. Like I said, I had just finished my sandwich and shoved the sandwich bag back into a brown paper sack when April walked up behind me and said, "May I sit with you, Brad?"

Now I wasn't surprised that she knew me. Everyone of consequence at Armwood knew me, Brad "Rock" Paxton, star six-one, 190 pound running back. If that sounds conceited, at the time conceit was barely adequate to describe my massive ego. Two years of being picked as the county's top running back--and the press that went with it--left me wallowing in self admiration. Time changed that as the reader will learn.

For April, it was quite different. She was a non-person in Armwood's social world. Pretty--but not yet beautiful--and a junior, she had many girl friends but no boy friends of note. There were several reasons for her low social status: she was new to the school, shy, a late bloomer in terms of physical maturation, and very bright. The latter attribute scared off most of the less gifted dudes.

So, when she asked if she could sit with me, it was a request that I acknowledged with interest. Her soft, throaty voice got to me right off, and I turned to look into her face, into her dark, long lashed eyes. For some reason--as I recall--I found myself fixated on her face, not her physical properties or lack thereof as I was wont to do. I did recognize her as the girl whose locker was three from mine on the same side of the hall. Of course, I noticed her as one notices a bump in the road, but I had never really looked at or spoken to her.

Anyway, I brushed some crumbs from the bench and said, "Help yourself, doll. You're?"

"April Perry. My locker is near yours," she said as she sat and opened her lunch box and took out half of a Subway sandwich.

"Yeah…I know. How'd you know my name…April?"

"Everyone knows you, Brad. I've seen you play several times." I noticed how long and delicate her fingers were as she lifted the sandwich to her mouth and nibbled off a corner. She was very dainty. I liked the way she stuck out her pinky. Framed by shoulder length, glistening black hair, her face was tanned and unblemished. She knew that I was staring at her. She blushed and--like magic--dimples appeared in her cheeks. I thought she had kissable lips, although I wasn't certain what made some lips kissable and some not.

"You're new here, April?"

"Yes. I started last fall." She nibbled off the other corner of her Subway "eat fresh" sandwich.

"What year you in…sophomore?"

"No. Junior."

"You look…uh…too young to be a junior."

3

"I was going to school in Zurich…Switzerland. When I returned to Florida, they tested me and advanced me a grade and a half."

"Wow. You've got to be a genius or something."

"Probably something," she said and smiled. "Maybe a geek."

The more we talked, the more I realized she was very special. And I realized something else. I needed to see her again. So I said, "You going to the prom?" It seemed impulsive, but it really wasn't. Hell, I had to face it. She'd hooked me using kissable lips and dimples as bait.

"I haven't been asked, Rock." Her eyes met mine, and my world became hers.

"Yes you have," I said. "I'm asking. Will you go with me?"

She made my day without hesitation. "Yes, I will. It would please me," she said, and I blushed. Me, Rock Paxton, the tough, all-county back who could have almost any girl he wanted, I blushed and knew why then. I know why now, ten years later. I was--in antique parlance-- smitten.

We had a few minutes left in the lunch period, and we used it to compare our tastes in music, TV, movies, etc. And, of course, we made arrangements for our first date.

* * *

Prom night, I picked April up at seven o'clock and promised a beautiful, mature version of April that I'd have her daughter home at one a.m. I made the promise after I was told three things that sealed the deal: April was only sixteen; this was her first *unchaperoned* date; and her father was very strict and would be waiting up. After her mother finished, April kissed her and said, "Enough, mother. You'll scare Rock away."

The beautiful lady's eyebrows arched at the mention of my hard won nickname. She stared at me and then at her daughter before shrugging and saying, "You kids have a good time, and remember...Rock...one a.m. sharp."

That night was the capper. She was more than I counted on. First off, she made me feel proud. When she was snubbed by several of my *old* girl friends, I became angry and she giggled. "It's nothing, Rock. They're jealous of me." She tilted her head and her dark eyes captured mine. And she added, "And I understand why they're jealous. You're very handsome, you know."

She was bubbly and intelligent. Knew more about most things--except football--than I did, and I didn't give a damn. It was great. And when it was over, I knew we belonged together. At 12:59 a.m. we arrived at the veranda of her magnificent home. She lifted her face for a goodnight kiss. Her lips were soft, cool and fresh. Kissable. Before she turned away, she touched my cheek with those slender fingers and whispered, "Don't forget about me, Rock. Please don't."

* * *

I wouldn't forget her. Couldn't. During the balance of June and part of July, we continued seeing each other daily. Even after ten-hour days laying concrete block for Dad's construction company, I'd make it to the Perry mansion. We'd spend an hour or two sitting on the broad steps of the veranda. Teasing. Laughing over private jokes. Holding hands. Sharing nonsense. We'd part after quick goodbye hugs and kisses. It was the best time of every day. It was always difficult to leave. But the time came for me to leave her. April. My girl. Neither of us knowing how long and painful the separation would be.

* * *

I had accepted a football scholarship from the University of Florida and was required to report for orientation and fall practice. Before leaving Tampa, I had secured April's promise to keep in touch. Even had her make a juvenile "cross my heart and hope to die" pledge not to date anyone else while I was in Tallahassee. I also pledged to stay clear of the literally hundreds of titillated coeds who would be waiting impatiently to make it with the "Rock."

As promised, we remained in touch. Constant touch. A month without her convinced me that I loved this slender, bubbly, bright child. I even thought about marrying her as soon as she was old enough. I wanted to lock her up for life. I had long since gotten over thinking I was doing her a favor and admitted I was her chattel. Yes, I loved this beautiful, intelligent child. Now, I think some of the attraction was paternal. Whatever it was, she was in charge. In charge of my present and my future. Love does that even to self-acknowledged heroes.

2

It was late August and the first day of school. The dismissal bell rang as April opened her locker to remove a book bag. After closing and locking the narrow cabinet, she turned to confront a tall, rangy boy-man who had a reputation for arrogance and aggressive, lewd behavior. Distaste washed over her face as he spread his bare, sinewy arms--like a point guard on defense--and moved with her from side to side as she tried to get by.

"What'sa matter, babe. Got no time to talk to a friendly classmate?" Crass and undisciplined, Josh Sampson was one of April's least favorite people. A pretty boy who believed looks alone guaranteed conquest, absent manners and reasonable intelligence.

"Please get out of my way, Josh. You shouldn't even be here. You've graduated."

"So what. Me and my friends thought we'd stop by and cheer up some of the babes we left behind."

"Please, Josh. I have volley ball practice." Josh grinned and instead of moving, he spread his arms around her and placed his hands flat against the wall of lockers. In back of Josh, four cronies watched their leader and smiled in unanimous appreciation of his *coolness*.

Josh pushed his face into hers. "How about a kiss, cutie. Show me how hot you are." Without hesitation, April slammed her fist into Josh's nose. A year on the volley ball team had developed substantial pop in her fisting technique. Blood spurting from his nose, he staggered back, caught his balance, and stepped forward to punish her. April ducked away from his clutching hands and swung her book bag in a wide arc. The bag, laden with books, caught Josh on the side of his head and sent him to his knees.

"You stuck up bitch," he screamed. "You little pig. I'll get you." As she walked away, he stood, reached into a pocket, pulled out a soiled handkerchief, and held it to his bleeding nose. Then he turned angrily to his grinning choir and stopped their derisive laughter by driving his fist into the stomach of the closest of the quartet--one Angelo Donato.

* * *

It was nine-thirty on a humid August evening a week later. Following choir practice, April left a side exit of the First Baptist Church of Brandon and entered the large parking lot. She had stayed behind the other choir members to rehearse a solo scheduled for the following Sunday morning. After saying goodnight, the choir director had left the building by another exit, which opened into a reserved parking area.

Although alone, April had no reason for anxiety, yet she found herself lengthening her strides across the lot. There were only two vehicles in the lot: her red Sebring and an old white Ford van sitting beside it. She'd never seen the van before. As she approached the Sebring, she thought it strange that---with all the available spaces--the van would take the one next to hers. She tried to shake off her apprehension as she walked between the two vehicles.

She opened the Sebring's door and prepared to slide in. She didn't make it. A sound from behind caused her heart to jump and hammer in her chest. Before she could turn, a pair of strong arms wrapped around her, pinning her arms to her sides. Another attacker gripped her head as a third shoved a cloth into her mouth when she opened her mouth to scream. She struggled to free herself from the hands holding her prisoner.

She heard the side van door slide open. And she heard a familiar voice say, "Take her car. We'll meet you there." Fright gripped her, but failed to immobilize her. She continued to fight. The man holding her from behind yelled when she slammed the back of her head into his nose. She was lifted from the pavement and thrown into the van. She tried to see faces. The parking lot lights revealed she was hostage to Richard Nixon, Ronald Reagan, Bill Clinton and--yes--Mickey mouse. The van driver wore no mask. Reagan sat on her chest while Nixon and Clinton piled in to help restrain her. Mickey closed the van door and stayed behind to drive her car.

A strip of tape over her eyes ended the need for disguises.

The van took off while she lay on musty carpeting struggling to breathe. She couldn't accept what she knew was going to happen and struggled until exhausted. In a trip prolonged by fear, April fought the horrible anticipation of what she knew would happen when the van stopped. With a bump when it cleared a curb, it did stop. The side doors slid open. She made one last futile effort to escape. Strong but not strong enough, she gave in as her clothing was ripped and cut from her body. Her mind traveled away from the reality of it. April Perry, a sophisticated child, experienced her first sex. Her sobs subsided as she was mauled and repeatedly penetrated by her attackers. Then it was over.

They dragged her, limp and exhausted, from the van and dropped her on the damp earth beside the Sebring. Laughing and pounding each other on the back and shoulders, they scrambled into the van and drove away from where she lay. Shivering, she drew her knees up and clutched them to her naked and bruised breasts. Then she passed out.

* * *

It was eleven-thirty when patrolman Rich Martino noticed the red Sebring parked in a vacant field just off of Fletcher Avenue. Tired and on the last leg of his patrol, he was tempted to continue on to his home a half mile away. A good cop, he resisted the temptation, and slowed to a stop. Turning on his spotlight, he swept the area around the vehicle. The powerful light easily penetrated the sparse vegetation and picked out the motionless body of a nude female.

Martino leaped from his patrol car and raced to April's side. He pulled out the cloth dangling from her mouth and removed the tape from her eyes. Her trauma was obvious. He returned to the cruiser and returned with a blanket. She groaned as he attempted to wrap the blanket around her. She cried out and attempted to crawl away, mumbling,

"Please…no more… please I hurt. No. Please." She tried to push his hands away.

"Take it easy, kid, I'm a police officer. Just let me cover you up."

"Police officer…you are…police officer?"

"Sure am, darling. Just let me cover you up, and I'll have you at the hospital in ten minutes." Empathy tore up the normally firm control of his emotions. He had seen a lot of evil during his sixteen years on the force, but this slender child's trauma shook him more than he wanted it to. *What kind of bastards could do this…to this child…this innocent child?* Was the question that ran through his mind as he carried her to the cruiser and gently placed her on the rear seat.

As he arranged the blanket over her, she said weakly, "They all raped me…Clinton, Reagan, Mickey Mouse, and Nixon…they hurt me…so bad. Why? Why?"

""I know they hurt you, kid. I know. Damn them."

After placing her in the cruiser, Martino called in and arranged for a crime scene unit to take over the site and her car. He concluded the conversation by saying, "The poor kid says she was raped by Clinton, Reagan, Nixon, and Mickey Mouse. No crap. Probably hallucinations. I'm surprised she didn't see Donald Duck, too. No I won't wait for crime scene people, this kid needs help now. Tell them to get their butts moving."

3

Detective Dewayne Jackson of the sex crimes unit got the call. Within ten minutes, he and his partner Luis Agosto were heading for Tampa General hospital. Dewayne was black, deep chested and broad shouldered. A strong and personable man on loan from homicide. A man on his way up. Agosto, a thin Hispanic, was rakishly handsome. His hair and neatly trimmed mustache were crisply white against his brown skin. Both enjoyed their work, each other, and a good argument.

"Who's the broad?" Luis asked.

"No broad, Luis. A young woman. A kid. You've got no respect."

"Where I grew up, all women were broads."

"Well, now you're grown and a few miles from where you grew up."

"Okay. Who's the princess, Galahad?"

"Very funny. What'd you do if someone called that sweet little daughter of yours a broad?"

"I'd put his ass down and make him eat dirt." A pause ensued before Luis asked, "Okay, partner. Who's the poor kid?"

"Kid named April Perry. Daughter of big time attorney Preston Perry."

"That sounds like trouble. I think the guy's a pal of the D A. Got big time political muscle. *Mucho influencia.*"

"Why you always throw in a little Spanish when we're having a serious discussion?"

"To impress you. I'm bi-lingual, you know. And I'll bet you don't know a single word of Swahili…or Watusi."

"You're full of it, you know. Give me one complete sentence in Spanish. Go ahead. Tell me what you had for dinner."

"So, I'm not fluent. But I am of Spanish heritage."

"Yeah. Fourth generation Floridian. You been here long enough to call yourself an American. Your great grandpa brought cigar making to Ybor City from Cuba."

"My great grandfather was a rancher."

"Yeah. He herded cigarillos and big black Cuban cigars." Dewayne smiled as they pulled into a reserved space at the emergency room entrance. "Behave yourself, Luis. The nurses are off limits. No touching."

"What else, *compadre*? I'm a married man."

"So? I hadn't noticed." He laughed and grabbed Luis' shoulder. Luis was one of the most firmly married people he knew. A mention of the word "adultery" and he'd make the Sign of the Cross and say three Hail Marys.

* * *

After a quick introduction and acknowledgement at the reception desk, the two detectives were passed through and directed to where April Perry was being treated. They arrived at the room and were greeted by a stern-faced Corporal Rich Martino who was guarding the door. "Lieutenant. I see you're still putting up with that white-haired old man."

"Watch yourself, Rich. A little respect for your elders, please." Only thirty-nine, Agosto was accustomed to the tease and went along with it, often referring to himself as "the old guy." Both detectives shook hands with Martino.

"How's the kid doing, Rich?" Jackson asked.

"Don't know yet, Lieutenant. She'd calmed down some by the time I got her here."

Jackson turned to a beautiful woman who was standing on one side of the door. "You're the girl's mother?"

"Yes. Maggie Perry." She'd been crying and hadn't finished. Turning to a man leaning against the wall on the other side of the door, Jackson asked, "And you're the girl's father...Preston Perry?"

"Yes," he answered abruptly.

Perry looked more like a stevedore than the head of an international law firm with offices in Tampa, Buenos Aires, Boston, London and Zurich. Square, thick shoulders topped his six-foot frame. From his shoulders to his feet--in body width and depth--he seemed to be of three dimensions. He was a human rectangle and appeared shorter than his actual six feet. A fringe of black hair ringed his bald pate. From his broad, high forehead to his square chin, his features spoke of power. Determination. Influence.

Except for the early amenities, silence prevailed outside the room where the hospital team would be using a rape kit and following the precise instructions required for its use by law enforcement. An hour passed before the door finally opened and two nurses and an MD walked out carrying a paper bag and a tray of capped and labeled test tubes.

Dewayne glanced at the MD's name tag and asked, "You're finished, Doctor Fermin?"

"Yes. And you are?"

"Lieutenant Jackson. TPD. Will it be all right to question the girl?"

"The girl's name is April." Preston Perry abruptly entered the conversation.

Ignoring Perry, Dewayne repeated his question in abbreviated form, "May we, Doctor?"

"After I do," Perry inserted himself between Jackson and Fermin. "No one talks to April 'til we agree on some ground rules."

Jackson placed a large hand on Perry's shoulder. "I know you're upset, Counselor. No one on God's earth could fail to understand that. But the sooner we interview…April… the sooner we'll have some facts to work with."

Perry wasn't finished. "Doesn't the damn department have a female detective who could interview rape victims?"

"We certainly have…and one will probably re-interview April in a day or two when she's feeling better. Now…Dr. Fermin?"

"I believe it's all right to interview her. She's had a light sedative. Perhaps her mother could accompany you…hold her hand. Take it easy, Detective. She's had a hellish experience."

Perry's fury had mounted. He wasn't used to being pushed aside. "Still don't understand why we can't get a woman out here instead of…"

"A black man?" A mischievous smile touched Jackson's lips.

"Don't exercise your damned paranoia on me, Jackson. I don't give a hot damn if you're black, white, brown, green, yellow, striped or checkered. I'd just prefer to have a woman…w-o-m-a-n…interrogate our girl."

Maggie Perry stepped in. "Preston…please. I'm sure the detective will be thoughtful. Please. I'll be with her."

"Okay, Maggie. The D A's on his way. The detective better be damn sure he respects April's feelings about what happened."

* * *

April lay on her side facing a wall when her mother sat down on a chair beside the bed. Maggie took her daughter's hand in one of hers and began to stroke her hair with the other. "Hello, sweetheart. Detective Jackson needs to ask you some questions. Are you okay with it?" There was a long silence before April nodded. "Good girl," her mother said and rewarded her with a kiss on the forehead.

"Thanks, April. How are you doing, youngster?" Jackson didn't anticipate the nature or tone of her response.

Slowly, deliberately, April turned her head and stared into Jackson's eyes. "I feel like a pig…a dirty pig. Have you ever…been…gang raped by a bunch…of slobbering, smelly animals, Mister Detective?"

"April. The detective understands how horrible it was for you."

"Does he? He's a man isn't he? Men rape. They don't get raped."

"April."

"Okay…mother…I guess…I'll be safe as long as you're here."

Dewayne shook off the intended put down. He smiled as he asked her to describe in as much detail as possible the events of the rape from the very beginning. There was another prolonged silence before she spoke again. Then, starting in a low monotone, she picked up speed and emotion as she got into the horror of the actual rape. Jackson used his own unique shorthand to keep up with her. He circled one entry several times: JshSmpsn. When April finished, she closed her eyes and sobbed softly.

Jackson shook his head and looked at Maggie Perry. Tears were streaming down her face again. "We'll get the filthy bastards. I promise you that."

"But will you be able to help April get over it?"

"That I can't promise, ma'am. Sorry. Perhaps in time… God only knows."

* * *

When Jackson emerged from April's interrogation, Luis pointed down the hall. "District Attorney Donatello is here. He wants us in the conference room to go over the ground rules. Perry's ground rules, I suspect."

"Bully. The big man really stood up to Perry."

"Yeah. He stood up. Like field corn stands up to a tornado." The detectives didn't care much for Miles Donatello. He was too political and made too many deals that let bad guys out too soon.

They entered the conference room. Perry was at the head of the rectangular table. On his left was Donatello. On the right, Dr. Fermin. Agosto and Jackson split up and sat facing each other across the table.

Perry began. "The district attorney and I have discussed this horrible incident. He has agreed that the detectives shall have the full force of his office behind them every step of the way. Whatever they need...expedited forensics... warrants. With his capable assistance...and with an aggressive, intelligent investigation...I can't believe that the five punks who desecrated my child will be on the street very long."

Perry paused long enough to stare at Jackson and Agosto. He continued, after being convinced that the detectives had gotten the message. "Now...once these animals are in custody...contacts shall be limited to attorneys...family members only if they're juveniles. All interrogations will be conducted by Agosto and Jackson. The press will be barred at all court appearances...since

April is only sixteen, this is appropriate. Now, one final thing. All parties to this should understand that I shall pursue all legal means to prevent word of this travesty from going beyond the parties directly involved. If it does leak, I will expend a large portion of my substantial wealth to find the person or persons responsible and sue them until they cry for mercy."

Donatello looked around the table. "I think you've covered all the bases, Preston. We'll depend on Dr. Fermin to relay your comments to the hospital staff who were involved, and I personally will see that our forensic people and Corporal Martino are advised of the need for silence… out of respect for Miss Perry's right to privacy."

4

It didn't take long for detectives Jackson and Agosto to get a line on Josh Sampson and his quartet of followers. As promised, forensics were processed in a hurry-up mode. Several things accelerated the investigation: The van used in the rape was recovered and found to have been stolen from a carpet contractor. A broken lock found near the firm's security gate had a clear thumb print on it's face. Josh Sampson's. Near where the van was recovered, a tire track was found. It matched the oversized right rear tire of Sampson's Chevrolet pickup. When Josh was brought in, he stonewalled even after a blindfolded April picked his voice from the voices of four detectives.

Josh's associates were quickly identified and brought in. When they were told of the evidence against their leader, they began to cave in. Pete Davidson, the youngest, was the first to admit being there, but said he didn't rape April because he couldn't *do it.*

Forensic evidence against them piled up: Semen specimens from April's body and the van's carpeting identified four of the five suspects. Blood from her head and blouse, which was recovered from the van, came from Davidson who also had a broken nose to show for his participation in the assault, if not the rape.

Within three weeks of the rape, faced with the mountain of physical evidence, Josh's other three companions followed Pete's example and agreed to testify against him. Confronted by his friends' treachery and the evidence, he also agreed to a deal after calling the others *pimps for the cops.*

After allocution, the sentencing of the five youths went according to the plea deals: Angelo Donato, Frank Pantereas, and Misha Pulaski--all 19 years old--received five to ten years; Pete Davidson, 18, got three to five; and Sampson, 19, ten to fifteen.

* * *

Preston Perry was subdued. From a couch in District Attorney Donatello's office, Perry expressed his displeasure. "They should have gotten double the time, Miles. The filthy animals."

"You were with me all the way on this, Preston. You wanted it quick and quiet. Limited exposure. At trial, we could have raised the ante, it would have increased the exposure. Even with gag orders, courtrooms leak like rusty barges."

"I know, Miles. Well, it's over. The stupid punks practically convicted themselves."

"Yes. Stupid and high on crack. When they get out, they'll be smarter and meaner. Especially Sampson. He'll have to be watched. Pretty boy with attitude."

Perry nodded and stood up and extended his hand to Donatello who came from behind his desk to walk his political ally to the door. "Yeah, it's over for them, Miles, but not for April, I'm afraid. Thanks for pushing this thing along."

"Any time, Preston. Keep in touch and…oh…how's April doing?"

"Too quiet for my liking. Maggie's worried, too. We're sending her to Boston to finish school. She'll probably stay there for college."

"Living with friends?"

"My sister Elaine. She heads up our Boston office. Elaine will be good for her…I think."

* * *

After the second scrimmage, I made what I still believe was a very wise decision. I decided to return home, never to visit Gainesville again…except as a spectator. Several factors prompted this decision. First, in that second scrimmage, a linebacker with the size and speed of a Humvee hit me in the open field after I'd gained exactly three yards and thought I was free to ramble. The tackle left me with a fractured right ankle and a touch more respect for the size and speed of collegiate linebackers.

Another notch in my decision came while I was sitting on the bench picking up splinters--a euphemism for being on inactive status when benches were made of pine. I had continued to attend practice despite my injury. For two weeks, I sat and watched three running backs I couldn't catch with a rocket in my rear consistently leave the Humvee grabbing for vapor trails. I could look forward to making the team as a *defensive* back in three or four years. My analysis was verified by the coach who said, and I quote, "Sorry you've decided to leave the program, Rock. You've got moxie and the kind of attitude we look for in a recruit. But you're right. Our recruiting year was the best we've had…especially at running back. We've got some real burners. I won't try to change your mind, son.

You've made some friends here and…hey…call for free tickets…any time. Good luck…uh…Paxton."

Short version of the coach's goodbye: "So long. It's been good to know you." Anyway he didn't shed any tears, and I was glad he didn't. Who wants to see a grown man with muscular ears cry?

I must admit at this point, that there was another pressing reason why I decided to leave Gainesville: I hadn't heard from April for three weeks. My calls to her home all resulted in a terse message: "I'm sorry but April is not available." I wasn't invited to call back. Her absence, not explained.

In desperation, I called my old coach at Armwood. He checked with the office and got back to me. April had dropped out of school. I sensed that something bad had happened.

So in early September, I hobbled to my car--a pickup truck on loan from my Dad's company. I jumped into the truck and made a speedy trip home, determined to get answers.

* * *

I left Gainesville at seven a.m. At nine, I lifted the iron ring on the front door and let it drop. A minute or so after the resounding "clunk" echoed through the big hall on the other side of the massive doors, a slender lady of forty or so opened the door. Wearing a gray dress with white apron and collar, her station in the household was clearly identified. She seemed amiable until I stated my mission. "I'm Brad Paxton. I'd like to see April…if she's available. Please."

Her face grew as cold as a Fargo icicle in February. She said, "I'm sorry, sir. But she isn't here." She started to close the door, but I stopped her by stepping onto the threshold.

"Can you tell me where she can be reached?"

"I'm sorry. All I can tell you is…"

"I'll take over, Dorothy." Maggie Perry touched the woman's shoulder and took her place. She held out her hand and said, "Hello, Rock. It's good to see you." Her eyes were rimmed with red tissue, and it wasn't allergy season.

"April…?"

"I'm sorry. Her father wanted her to finish high school at an academy in New England. You know…to prepare her for an Ivy League university."

"New England? Last time we talked she never said anything about leaving Tampa…going away to school."

"It was a rather quick decision…you know how her father is when he decides to do something. Maggie tried to smile and didn't make it.

"Could you give me an address? A phone number? I'd like to talk to her."

Tears came to her eyes. "I'm sorry, Rock. She's just settling in and…"

"What is it Mrs. Perry?"

"It's best that you leave. April doesn't want to hear from you, Rock. If she changes…her mind…I'll call you. I have your number. Please…leave, dear. Please."

"What's happened, Miz Perry…Maggie. Please tell me. Maybe I can help…do something. She's my girl. She'll always be my girl."

She sobbed and turned away. Nana of the north stepped in. I stepped away as she closed the door. All uncertainty had been dispelled, and now I was damned certain something bad had happened.

* * *

During the year following my return from Gainesville, I drove by the Perry residence almost daily. When rain kept me from working, I'd park up the street for hours, watching tradesman, mail persons, and members of the household come and go. The hope she'd return home died in a mist of despair. I finally accepted the fact that all I had of April--perhaps all I'd ever have--was a tear-stained prom picture that sat--still sits--on my bedroom dresser. My tears, of course. A sad but honest testimony to my distress over the loss of my first and only love.

PART TWO

Eight years after the beginning

Love never gives up,
Never loses faith,
Is always hopeful,
And endures through
Every circumstance.
1 Corinthians 7:13

5

Eight years after the beginning: During the eight years after April exited my life, she never left my thoughts for long. One thing I need to emphasize: Early on, I convinced myself that I could never love anyone the way I loved April. An obsession? I suppose. But I knew no one could replace the slender child with raven hair and long-lashed brown eyes who had turned me into her chattel on our first date. I don't know if many men--if any--fall in love to stay in love at eighteen. I did. Or thought I did.

I had dates over the years. Always disappointing.

The dates were part of a search--a longing--that had no resolution. Several extended relationships fizzled. It hadn't been the women. Most had been attractive, bright, accomplished. It had been me and I knew it then. I know it now. I still made trips past the Perry house when I was in the area. Hope had ended. Only nostalgia remained. That and the tear-stained 5 x 7 prom picture that sat on my dresser.

After passing on my gridiron career and leaving the University of Florida, I attended the University of South Florida in Tampa and graduated in three years with a degree in law enforcement, Criminology major. I paid my own way by working for dad part time. After graduation, I applied for the Tampa Police Department, was accepted, and graduated second in my cadet class. Dad was very proud, and after a total of four years of preparation, I felt ready to become Tampa's equivalent of Gotham city's legendary crime fighter. Look out crooks. Rock the enforcer is coming.

* * *

I got my first assignment riding with Sergeant Rich Martino, a big, florid faced guy from Georgia. He had a ton of experience and a sense of humor, seemingly not diminished by that experience. On our third night together, we were patrolling on the city's north side. The first four hours had been about as exciting as watching concrete harden.

We'd stopped at a Dunkin' Donut shop, eaten a pair of cream filled jobs, and were drinking our second cups of coffee when Rich broke a period of silence. "I got to wondering about something when I heard you were breaking in with me, Brad."

"Wondering about what?"

"What happened to you at Florida?"

"Happened?"

"Yeah. Followed your career at Armwood. Rock Paxton, all county running back. Heard you were going to U of F. Then nothing."

"There was nothing after that."

"Nothing?"

"I went, stayed six weeks and came home."

"Didn't like it?"

"Didn't like the fractured ankle I got in my second scrimmage…and didn't like the fact there were three RB's who were better than I was. Bigger. Faster. All ran a 4.4 forty or better. I accepted the fact that I wasn't good enough and came home."

"So you gave up. No more Rock?"

"Gave up? Yeah, guess I did. I was out for the season and over-matched. And I'd left a girl behind that I needed to see."

"A girl?"

"Yeah. Maybe you've heard of her father. He…" The call came in before I could finish. We dumped our coffee on the pavement and wheeled out of the lot. Our destination, a jewelry store break-in four blocks from our location.

* * *

Bridge light flashing, we wheeled to the curb just as an alarm bell tore the night silence to shreds. Simultaneously, the Sergeant and I slid from our seats and crouched behind our open doors with guns drawn. I watched and tried to listen as Rich grabbed the mike and called for backup. A shadow stepped from the doorway alcove. One man with hands raised. I picked him up with our spotlight. He shouted something I couldn't understand because of the alarm's raucous clanging. I barely heard the shot, but I saw the results: The look of surprise on the man's face; the sudden fall backward; and the red stain spreading over his chest. He dropped to his knees before falling face down on the sidewalk.

I glanced across the seat at Martino, and he was looking at me, a scowl on his face. I guess I was scowling also. I shouted over the alarm, "Why'd you shoot, Sarge? The man was giving up. His hands were raised. Hell, he didn't want to die."

* * *

A security service cop and the store owner showed up together and turned off the alarm. Finally, we could communicate without shouting. We were standing over the dead man and Martino shook his head and asked a very pertinent question. "Who the hell shot him…and why? You say you didn't fire your weapon, and I believe it. And I sure as hell didn't fire mine. So who and why?"

The question was rhetorical, but I answered anyway… being a rookie and all. "A partner to shut him up?"

"And where was this partner? He wasn't in the store since the man was shot in the chest." Martino looked across the street where a phone booth was illuminated by a street light. "Let's look over there, Rock."

We crossed over as the lights from several official vehicles illuminated the area. We searched the ground around the phone booth, and I spotted a shell casing. Martino held up his massive right hand as I bent over to retrieve it. "Let the crime scene folks do that, Rock." Then he shouted in a booming voice that rattled the booth's glass and aluminum frame. "Hey. Forensics…Agnes. You guys get your butts over here."

"Who's Agnes?"

"Agnostic Broadhurst. Damn good crime scene investigator."

"Agnostic? One hell of a name. Is he…?"

"An agnostic? No way. Bible's his handbook for living. Mother wanted a girl…was going to name her Agnes. When a boy showed up, she named him agnostic to get even. He's kept the name to get even with her."

* * *

The night wasn't over for Martino and me. We wrote our reports and turned our weapons in. Since the would-be burglar was dead and didn't have a weapon, we'd be on administrative leave until slugs from our weapons were compared to the one in his chest. Sitting at a table in the break room, we discussed what had happened while drinking coffee that tasted as though it had been shipped from Saudi Arabia in a tanker. It was that bad.

Martino became suddenly quiet. "What's up Sarge? You worried about something?"

"Not worried…something about that guy's face. I know the face but can't place it."

For fifteen minutes, I waited while he sat staring at the ceiling, flipping through his mental Rolodex for the dead man's identity. Tired of waiting, I asked, "Can we leave, Sarge? I'm bushed."

"Yeah…before we get picked up for loitering or get rushed to Tampa General to get our stomach's pumped." He smiled and tapped his half-empty cup.

As we left the building, Martino stopped and snapped his fingers, "I've got it."

"What? Jock itch?" I could be funny, too.

"The guy's name. Pete Davidson. One of the bastards who was in on that Perry kid's rape."

6

That Perry kid's rape. It was a fist in the gut. My legs turned to gelatin. "What rape? What Perry kid?" I muttered. I knew the answer. I finally knew what bad thing had happened. The bad thing I could not be told.

"The lawyer's kid. Preston Perry's kid...five punks... hey, Rock what the hell's wrong? Your face is white. Here. Sit down. I'll get some water." Sarge helped me as I sank to the bench in front of my locker. Eight years since I'd seen her, and it was as though I had heard something that had happened yesterday. Sarge returned with a cup of water, which I took with trembling hands. "Tell me…about it, Sarge. Tell me what happened."

"I see. You knew her." It wasn't a question.

"She…April…she was my girl…for a very short period of time."

"Damn, Rock, I'm sorry. You never heard about it?"

"No…it had to have happened while I was in Gainesville. That's when I stopped hearing from her. When her family stonewalled me about where she was. I'm okay now. Just tell me what happened. I need to know."

"It wasn't nice, Rock. Happened…let's see…eight years ago in August. Be best forgotten. Knowing the details won't…"

"Please, Sarge."

"I was the one who found her. In a vacant lot off Fletcher Avenue. She was lying beside her car…undressed… bruised…bleeding."

"Bastards. The filthy bastards."

"They were that. She was just a kid. I wrapped her in a blanket and took her to Tampa General. Met her parents there. Tore them up."

"There were five of them?"

"Yeah. Five. The guy got shot tonight…Davidson…said he wasn't involved in the actual rape. I guess he wasn't. Others confirmed it."

I swallowed hard, trying to avoid the thought of four guys piling on April. "How lucky for her...lucky only four guys raped her." I clenched my hands, stared at my knuckles, and thought how great it would be to smash their faces to red meat. "Where are they? I assume they were convicted. Are they still in prison?"

"As far as I know, three got five to ten. They're probably out. The alpha male got ten to fifteen."

"This leader of the pack...who was it?"

"Wise-ass pretty boy named Sampson."

"Josh Sampson?"

"Yeah, Josh. You knew him?"

"Kicked his butt in ninth grade for stealing a kid's lunch money. Jerk bought cigarettes with the money at lunchtime and blew smoke in the poor kid's face."

"Maybe that's why he...well..."

"Why he went after April?"

"Punks like him can hold grudges."

"Other guys can hold grudges."

"Guys like you?"

"Your damned right. Guys like me."

"Don't y'all do anything stupid, Rock. They've done... or are doing...their time. They'll get theirs...you know, having a record and all."

"They didn't get enough time...a maximum of fifteen years for a gang rape of a sweet kid like April? Give me a break. Damn their souls to hell." I spit out the words as though they were coated with lye.

"Old man Perry wanted it handled quick and quiet. The best way to do that was to make deals they couldn't refuse…that's what I heard. It was very hush hush."

"I heard later her family sent her away to school. That's what I heard. Not sure about that either."

"They sent her to New England. That's all the family would tell me."

Martino sat on the bench beside me and put his huge arm over my shoulders. Neither of us spoke for perhaps five minutes. He broke the silence.

"Hey. I just remembered something that could take your mind off smashing faces…might cheer you up some."

"Fat chance, but go on."

"She's back in Tampa…working in the D A's office. You might want to look her up…for old time's sake." Sarge smiled.

"Who's back? April's back in Tampa?"

"Yeah. I had to testify a couple weeks back. She was second chair at the prosecutor's table."

How can one's emotional mindset go from mutilated to exhilarated in a second or two? That's what happened to me. *I might want to see her?* I leaped up from the bench and headed for the exit.

"What's your hurry, man? The courthouse doesn't open 'til ten a.m.," Sarge teased as he followed me from the locker room.

7

Sarge and I were put on leave until a hearing that would occur after they dug the bullet out of Pete Davidson's chest and compared it to slugs from our weapons. It was a pro forma activity designed to protect the department from accusations, like maybe they were covering up a bad shooting. *Tampa Tribune* and *St. Petersburg Times* reporters are not unlike porcine creatures who root in garbage until they find something succulent to chew on. The press would be nosing around, perhaps at the Davidson family's instigation after prompting by a lawyer with the odor of green in his nostrils.

I arose that first morning intending to spend some time in the courthouse lobby in the hope *she* would walk by. Eight years had passed, but I'd forgotten nothing about her. Impatient to be on the move, I ate my Cheerios staring at the only thing I had of her: The 5 x 7 prom picture in a silver frame. She had been beautiful, gentle, fun to be with; and eight years hadn't changed my feelings. Not even a violent rape could damage the image I carried in a special corner of my mind. It was a corner where she giggled, teased, and touched my cheek with her long, slender fingers. How could those punks have violated such an innocent, exquisite child? I asked that question of myself a dozen times that morning…or so it seemed. As my final response to that haunting question, I threw the half-eaten bowl of cereal into the sink and delighted at its destruction. Not bothering to stop and clean up the mess, I grabbed a jacket and headed for the court house.

* * *

I spent the morning sitting on a lobby bench reading the newspaper and hoping to catch April. This was after I called the D A's office and was told she was in court. Noon came. I folded the paper--which I'd read at least three times--and went to lunch. I returned to the courthouse and reclaimed the bench I'd abandoned fifteen minutes earlier. Barely an hour later, an elevator door opened across the lobby. There she was. Mature now. Still beautiful. Tall and slender, her raven black hair cut short, she walked toward me heading for the exit doors. I stood. She wore dark sunglasses, and I couldn't tell if she was looking at me. I lifted my arms to embrace her. Then dropped them as she passed me with no sign of recognition.

Perhaps she hadn't recognized me. It had to be the dark glasses. I couldn't believe she'd deliberately snub me. Not the Rock. I followed her through the door and onto the sidewalk. When I got close enough, I called, "April. April. It's me...Rock...Brad Paxton. Please stop. I need to talk to you."

She stopped and slowly turned. Irritation imprinted her smooth, tanned cheeks. "Okay, Brad. Say what you've got to say. I'm really very busy...don't have much time to waste these days."

Waste? Time taken to stop and talk to me was a waste? My exuberance became misery. She had seen me and walked by. Emboldened by a sudden flood of anger, I stared into her hostile face and responded. "Sorry I bothered you, April. I won't waste your time...God forbid. But for the record...if nothing else...I loved you eight years ago...have never stopped loving you. It's obvious I'm one of your bad memories. If you ever get over what turned you against me...I'll be there as your friend or your...oh...what the hell." I turned to walk away, then stopped, and said to her back, "It might cheer you up to learn that one of the punks who raped you got killed last night. Pete Davidson caught one in the chest. Make you happy, April? Does it?"

She walked to a valet driven car parked at the curb. The valet got out, took the tip she handed him and closed the door. She was gone. Again. I don't need to say this, but I will. I hated the punks who had destroyed what she had been. One was dead. Perhaps the others…well…that was a thought for another day.

8

Attorney Preston Perry laid the *Tampa Tribune* aside, and smiled across the breakfast table at his wife. Maggie was still very beautiful. Only forty-three, she looked younger--perhaps five-to ten years younger. Yes, during the eight years since April was raped, time had been kind to her mother--physically kind. But Maggie had never shaken off the deep depression that followed the brutal attack. She had frightening mood swings. Sometimes gay and charming. Sometimes violently angry. She often became a stranger to reality. Avoided it. One of her out-of-touch expectations came in the form of a challenge for him to do the *right thing* and kill the men who'd raped their virgin daughter.

Not a man inclined to admit mistakes, sometimes Perry acknowledged to himself that it might have been a mistake to send April to Boston. Maggie had strenuously objected at the time, saying if April ever needed her, it was in the months following the rape. April's departure had been followed by crying jags that sometimes lasted for days.

April's decision to lease a condo upon her return to Tampa further disrupted Maggie's emotional equilibrium. Medications had reduced her mood swings somewhat, but Preston never knew for certain who would appear at the breakfast table.

Taking a chance that he had some news that would please her, he said, "One of them got it the other night."

"Who got what, dear?"

"Pete Davidson…one of the animals who attacked April…he got shot outside a jewelry store he broke into."

"Shot? Killed?"

"Yes."

"They should all be dead by now, don't you think?"

"There was something unusual about it." He jumped in, anticipating the direction of her thoughts.

"And what was unusual?"

"A 911 call reported a burglary in progress, but the alarm didn't go off until a squad car arrived five minutes later."

"The police...shot him?"

"No...at least the cops say no. They won't say much, but the word is Davidson got it when he walked out of the store with his hands up. Someone shot him from across the street."

"Was it you?"

"Me?"

"You weren't home the night before last."

"I had a meeting with...good Lord, Maggie. Are you inferring that I killed the man?"

"If you didn't, you should have...I don't know why you refuse to do the manly thing and kill those animals...like they put down a horse with a broken leg or a mad dog."

"Maggie, I'm an officer of the court. I'm on the side of the law."

"I don't think people like that should be protected by the law."

"God, I don't know how to respond to this...I hope you aren't telling others that you expect me to...good Lord. What can I say?"

"Don't worry, dear. My lips are sealed. Let's just say some nice person...a very courageous one...did it for you." Maggie smiled, winked and dabbed her lips with a napkin.

Preston shook his head in disbelief but continued. "Police have a murder to solve now. Hope they don't work too hard looking for the person who pulled the trigger. Deserves a medal."

"Yes those who punish evil need to be rewarded." She winked again and he realized she was flirting. Offering him compensation for his bravery?

After a period of silence, Preston said, "I forgot to mention…one of the two cops on the scene was Rock Paxton."

"Rock Paxton is a policeman now?"

"It seems so."

"Rock was so sweet to April. Such a handsome young man."

"The other cop was named Martino…I'll be damned… Martino was the name of the big cop who found April that night. Remember him? He stood at the door while they took care of April. Corporal Dick…no…Rich Martino." Perry glanced at the newspaper article. "Yeah, Rich Martino. The same guy."

"Strange don't you think?" Strange that the police officer who helped April that night and Brad…who loved her so much…would be there when this Davidson fellow got shot?"

"Let's change the subject, dear. I meant to ask if April will be here for Thanksgiving."

"I don't think so, Preston. She said she had some work to do...and afterwards she might go to the beach and relax."

"Damn...that's horse crap," he erupted. "Doesn't she know Elaine's coming in from Boston? Bringing mom?"

"Don't you dare be angry. It's your fault she's become so alienated. Sending her away...when she needed me...and I needed to be with her. It's your fault she's grown so cold inside...like you...and like Elaine. Like all lawyers."

He pushed back from the table. "My fault? My fault that she has no more feeling than a potato? Elaine's fault? Our fault because we're lawyers? God knows I still love her... and you beyond description. But I won't take any more of this crap. It's one person's fault. And that person's name is April Perry. She stopped feeling that night...and even with the best treatment and Elaine's love...she remains an emotional cripple...damn. Why take it out on us? In order to heal, perhaps she needs to kill the rest of them. I'm going to the office, Maggie. I'll be home late."

9

Captain Dewayne Jackson--the newly appointed head of The Major Crimes Bureau--smiled across his desk at his old partner, Luis Agosto, acting head of homicide. "You still making like a detective, Luis?"

"In my spare time. I spend most of my waking hours trying to figure out what got you promoted to Bureau head…with only twenty-five years of service."

Jackson laughed and looked at Sarge and me. We'd been called for a sit down with Agosto in his office. "Paxton, this skinny refugee from a cigar factory is Detective

Lieutenant Luis Agosto, my partner for more years than I care to remember. Rich, you know Luis, I believe." After the introduction, Jackson continued, "Luis caught the Davidson case…wanted to hear what went down from the guys who answered the call. I suggested you meet here… since I have a meeting with the Major." Jackson stood and walked to the door. He took his hat from a wall hook and said, "I'll leave you two in Luis' hands and…Luis?"

"Yes, Captain."

"Use my chair in my absense, but don't get any wild ideas. Using my chair is one thing, but taking over is another. The Major and I are joined at the hip."

"Right. I've suspected that ever since the word got out about your rapid rise to power." The Captain laughed again as the door closed behind him. "He's a great guy," Luis added when certain his friend was out of hearing.

Agosto walked behind the desk and assumed *the* chair. Serious now, he pulled a note pad from an inside jacket pocket. He leafed through the pages until he found what he wanted. "Okay, fella's, I want each of you to recount what happened on the night in question. You first, Sergeant."

Sarge started and did as instructed in great detail. I followed and my report only differed in the use of a verb variant or two. When we finished, Agosto frowned and said, "Remarkable. You two haven't been rehearsing have you?"

Sarge and I protested simultaneously. Agosto smiled and said, "Kidding guys. Good reports. Now, I've read the crime scene situation reports...schematics and so forth...the forensic information, and conducted several interviews. You deserve to be filled in. I'll go over what we have...which isn't a helluva lot. First, the 911 call came in exactly six minutes before you arrived on the scene and called for backup. We think the gunner knew exactly where you were and how long it would take you to show. As you suspected, the call was placed from the booth across the street from the jewelry store."

"Sounds like Davidson might have been set up," Sarge said.

"Also sounds as though the shooter may have wanted us blamed for the shooting," I said.

"Two things. We do think he was set up. And we're not sure it was a guy."

"Could have been woman? Damn good shot for a woman."

"Sexist," Agosto said. "The caller's voice was disguised by the use of something like tissue paper over the end of a tube...falsetto...911 recording had a buzzing sound... sounded like one of those toys kids hum on... wazoos."

"Kazoos," I corrected.

"Yeah, Kazoos. So that gives us someone...man or woman...waiting until you guys show."

"Maybe a partner who chickened out," I said weakly.

"No. I think it someone who wanted him dead and wanted to make a show of the execution."

"What would be the motive? Was he involved in drugs?" Sarge asked.

Agosto responded, "Not that we can determine. No problems with the law since the rape. Since he got out five years ago, he's had a steady job...no arrest record whatsoever. Clean as a whistle for five years. Family, friends, and employer defend him. Say he learned his lesson. Was sincerely sorry for his part in the rape."

"No known enemies, no illegal activities...but someone hated him enough to set him up and kill him." I said as something trickled into my mind. Something I didn't want to consider.

"One final thing. Did you two hear any shots before the one that took him out?"

I looked at Sarge and he looked at me. We both shrugged. "Why?" Sarge asked.

"The store owner found evidence of damage inside the store. We found two slugs. I think the first two shots were fired as you approached... fired through the door to set off the alarm. We believe now, that Davidson was there to meet someone, not to break in."

"And the someone he was there to meet was the someone who put him down," I said.

"Good thinking, Rock. I like that cop talk. 'Put him down' sounds just like the TV cops…like Stabler on Law and Order."

He was putting me down, so I took a chance on a payback. "You watch the show, too, Lieutenant? I thought your investigative techniques sounded familiar."

Sarge appeared shocked, but Agosto laughed, "Your buddy's got testiculos, Sarge. I like him."

"So what do we have? Someone hates this relatively docile character enough to devise a convoluted plan to kill him and make it look as though he was killed in the process of a break-in by a couple of trigger-happy cops. A plan that put the killer in jeopardy. Or, do we have a killer whose hate goes so deep that he or she wants an audience for the execution?" Agosto looked for a response from one of us.

Sarge did the honors. "In the first scenario, the killer would have to be stupid. Have to know the scheme wouldn't hold up under investigation. And like you said, Lieutenant, why put yourself in jeopardy? Doesn't make sense."

"What's your take, Brad.?"

"Perhaps the killer is a very bright person who wants to look stupid. Essentially, I agree with the second scenario… about the hate and the audience…but the first could also be in play."

"Good point. And I agree. My biggest problem…as with any investigation…is motive. I ask myself what has this guy ever done to warrant being executed?"

Good question, I thought. The premonition I'd had earlier had finally worked its way into the discussion. I felt I had to say it. "The rape of April Perry," I said. "That generated a lot of hate."

"You got it, Rock. Someone in the family, a friend, or the girl…the woman herself…has held this hate inside for eight years."

"But why wait eight years?" I asked.

"Davidson was inside for some of the time. And the girl…April Perry…is back in town after being away for most of that time," Sarge said, then looked at me and added, "Sorry, Rock."

For just a second, I hated Sarge. But he was telling it like it was. There was one thing I had to say, and I said it while thinking it could be the only reason I was there. "What about me as a suspect?"

"And why you, Paxton?" Agosto's dark eyes bored into mine.

"She was my girl. I loved her, and I believe that the punks who raped her deserve to die."

10

Two months following my sit down with Sarge and the Lieutenant, I received a request to report to Captain Jackson. I got there ten minutes early and was escorted to his office by a buxom, blue-eyed blonde with a great smile and flirty eyes. She knocked on the Captain's door and opened it after an invitation to do so.

"Captain, Patrolman Paxton is here for his appointment."

"Good. Come in, Paxton." I entered as the clerk closed the door behind me. "You're a little early, son. I'm expecting Lieutenant Agosto to join us. We can chat 'til he gets here."

"Yes, sir."

"Talked to the Major the other day about you. Seems he followed your football career at Armwood…had a daughter in the band. Anyway, he said you were a helluva tough guy."

"That was good of him," I said. What else could I say? This was going somewhere, and I had no idea where that somewhere was.

"Said in one game you got knocked silly by a guy the size of a water buffalo and got carried off the field. Said you came back in two plays later and ran forty yards for a TD."

"I recall the hit, Captain. I don't remember going back in. I must have been unconscious or insane. Probably the latter."

The Captain was still laughing when the Lieutenant came in. "You telling jokes again Captain?" As he sat down, he glanced at me and said, "You don't have to laugh, Paxton. It encourages him, and he always forgets the punch line."

"Watch it Luis, I'll have you brought up for insulting a superior."

"Superior? Oh, you mean in rank."

"See how insolent fourth generation cigar rollers can be when they have tolerant friends in high places?" All laughed. A short hiatus brought the repartee to an end. It was time for business.

"Paxton, I'm sure you're wondering why you're here." The Captain waited for me to respond.

"Yes sir."

"Yes. We in department administration have been throwing around some ideas on how to improve recruiting and training of young, talented personnel…specifically in Major Crimes. We've come to believe that moving guys up from the ranks after they've polished the seat of their pants…and the old apple…for a few years is a waste of time and talent. How does that strike you?"

"Sounds interesting." At that point, I understood where the meeting was going and couldn't pretend otherwise.

"Before we started a program of recruiting people off the street, it seemed that we should screen our younger personnel…in all divisions…and see what we had. You follow me?"

"Right with you, Captain."

"Based on some preliminary criteria, we identified ten possible candidates. Then applied more stringent criteria to the ten, and guess what? You came out looking like a daisy on a manure pile…so to speak. A degree in criminology. Number two in your cadet class. Scored well on aptitude tests and personality profiles…and last of all…you hit it off with one of our better detectives. Don't smile, Luis. If he's interested, you're going to have the responsibility to turn this rookie into a top drawer detective. A veritable bloodhound. You willing to be a guinea pig in this Detective Intern program, Rock?"

"Willing and eager, Captain. Sounds great."

"Okay. You take it from there, Luis."

"Right. You'll be my partner for an eighteen-month internship, Rock. Everywhere I go, you go. You'll be required to attend a dozen or so in-service training classes at the University of Tampa and USF. Most will be on your time, but at the Department's expense. I'll submit progress reports every three months. And progress will be expected. I may cut you some slack at first…but in the end…I'll be totally objective. You understand all of that, Rock?"

"Yes, sir."

"You still interested?"

"You bet. When do I start?"

"Right now." Luis handed me a small silver shield. With the stamped imprint: TPD - Detective Intern. They were prepared for an acceptance, by me or someone else.

I looked at the little silver badge, then at the Captain, then Agosto.

"I really appreciate the opportunity. And I won't let either of you down." Of course, at the time I didn't fully realize how difficult it would be to keep that promise.

* * *

Agosto and I left the Captain's office after handshakes all around. He led me to the squad room where a desk was waiting. Luis went to the reception area and returned with the blond whose name badge said Sheila Adams. She was carrying an armload of supplies. The usual stuff: note pads, pens, pencils, file folders, standard forms, etc.

"You want me to put things away for you?" Sheila asked, showing her white, even teeth. I found myself comparing her to April. Not as tall. Not as slender.

"No thanks, Sheila. Appreciate the offer, though."

"You're perfectly welcome, Rock. Anytime."

After Sheila left, Agosto went to his small office, and returned with a case file, which he laid on my desk. "Look through this, Rock. You have comments…questions… write them down. Take your time. We'll talk first thing tomorrow. Uh…by the way…I should mention you'll probably get some…looks."

"Looks?"

"Yeah, by guys who think you got a leg up. Think you're connected. Don't worry about it…they'll come to love you in time. Love runs rampant around here. See you manana, compadre."

The Lieutenant left and I opened the file. The item on top was an 8x10 photo of April as she'd been over eight years earlier. I stared at the photo much too long, finally setting it aside with a knot in my throat and an empty feeling in my gut. The second item didn't help. It was a report of a firearm purchase by Preston Perry. The form was dated in August, the year of the rape. The caliber matched that of the weapon that killed Pete Davidson. When Perry was questioned, he said he'd misplaced it. Had no idea what had happened to it.

My exuberating over my new assignment faded. I leaned back in my chair and stared through the closest window at nothing. Why did they make this move? Why put me with Agosto. To test my objectivity? Could I be objective? Would I need some slack?

11

Agosto stopped at my desk the next morning. Without preliminaries, I asked, "Why me on this case, Lieutenant?"

"It sort of bothers you, Rock? Thought it might. A few weeks ago, the Major…knowing I needed a new partner… came to the Captain and me with the idea of starting a Detective Intern program in Major Crimes. We batted around some ideas, and it came down just like the Captain described it…you know…the screening and all. And, to be honest, because of your history with the Perry family…we discussed taking the number two man from the screening. But I said, push comes to shove, I'll take Rock. When we went to the Major with our selection, his face lit up like Raymond James Stadium on a game night. You have a friend in a high place, Rock."

"Knowing the baggage I carry, why'd you take me over the guy who came in second?"

"To be frank…and don't let this go to your head…during our sit down after the Davidson hit, you impressed me. Martino knows both you and the guy who placed second, so I asked him what he thought. He said he favored you in terms of guts, brains, analytical ability, common sense, ambition, and determination. I admire Sarge…guy has turned down desk promotions because he likes what he does. Says he has a chance to do some good out there. So here you are, and we've got work to do."

"I like Sarge, too, Lieutenant. I don't plan on disappointing him," I said before going on. "I finished reading the file last night, and I do have a few questions."

"Ask away."

"The gun thing. Preston Perry says he misplaced it. Doesn't know where it is."

"We're going to clear that up today…I believe."

"Then…you've interviewed the other four guys involved in the rape. April and her father. Sounds as though you're focusing on everyone connected in any way. As I said before. Why not me? She was my girl."

"You have a pretty good alibi, being one of the responding officers."

"I could have had an accomplice."

"You could have…but I checked you out pretty good… talked to your friends, family…hey…your dad is a horse. What a man."

I shook my head, "Okay. And you interviewed Sampson outside. I can' t believe he's on the street."

"Believe it. He's out. Early release. Seems like a couple of inmates got a guard in a closet and were beating the hell out of him. Sampson heard the ruckus, dragged the other two inmates out and put them down. Probably saved the guard's life."

"Doesn't sound like the Sampson I knew. Only one he'd have guts enough to put down would be his grandmother… probably has."

"Don't believe he's the Sampson you knew, Rock. He's had a muscle makeover…got muscles on his eyelids. Spent half his time inside pumping iron."

"So….he's out…early release for saving the guard's butt?"

"That's it."

"Anyone think it might have been a set up? Two buddies bang the guard, and Sampson...like Superman...comes to the rescue."

"I thought about it...but I wasn't in the loop. No one asked me."

"And...from what I read...his PO says he's been a veritable angel since he got out. His employer is pleased with his work."

"You got it, partner. Anything else?"

Yes. What're we doing this morning?" I stood and removed my jacket from the back of my chair.

"We...my young intern...we've scheduled an interview with the lovely Counselor April Perry." I followed him to the exit, pulling on my jacket as I went.

* * *

Noting my apprehension as we approached the door to April's office, Agosto stopped and said, "This is probably a tough go for you, Rock. If you don't mind, I'll do the interview. You take notes. Stiff upper, amigo."

I didn't mind a damned bit and said so.

April didn't stand as we entered her office. She simply motioned toward two chairs that had been placed in front of her desk. She glanced at me, at Agosto, and said, "It's your quarter, Lieutenant."

"Of course, Counselor. We won't take much of your time. We're having a problem with the weapon thing.

You know…the S&W Astra model your father purchased shortly after you were…uh…attacked. It's very possible that it's the weapon that killed Pete Davidson. You being a prosecutor…and all…must realize the suspicion it places on your dad. The only way we can clear this up is to locate the weapon in question and do ballistic comparisons."

"So why come to me? If Dad says it's lost, it's lost."

"Well…it's this way, Counselor. Your father buys a gun shortly after … uh…"

"I was raped by the Sampson five?"

"Yes. Thank you. Then he sends you to Boston… probably to save you from possible embarrassment. So… being a father of a lovely daughter…I asked myself what I might do if she were raped, and I was sending her away to protect her from gossip."

"Yes?"

"I came up with the thought that I might buy her some protection…a firearm…and give it to her as a *bon voyage* gift."

"Very astute, Lieutenant. I didn't want the thing, but he insisted. He also asked my Aunt Elaine to have me instructed in the use of the weapon…after I got to Boston."

"Why would he lie…do you think?"

"Now, that's not astute, or maybe it wasn't astute for a reason."

"I'm not that devious, Counselor. The reason?"

"To prevent suspicion for the Davidson killing from falling on me. That seems obvious. He simply tried to protect me."

"Do you believe he thinks you might have killed Davidson?"

"I won't pretend to know what my father thinks, but he's never suggested that I was a murderer."

"So, Counselor, did you learn to shoot the weapon?"

"Yes. I became very proficient…for a woman."

"And where is the weapon now?"

"I have no idea. I left it with some old clothes, notebooks, books and stuff when I left the university."

"These things were left at your Aunt's place?"

"No. At an apartment I leased near the campus."

"Could we have the address of that apartment?"

"Of course. But I came home almost a year ago. I doubt if any of the things I left behind are still there."

"You're probably right, but we will check."

"I hope you find the gun."

"Yes. Me too. It would clear up some very pertinent questions. By the way, Counselor, don't you believe it was very careless…you know…you leaving a dangerous weapon where it could be found and used in a crime?"

"Yes it was. I was very stupid."

"Somehow, I don't see you doing something *very stupid*, Counselor," Agosto said as he pushed his chair back and stood.

"Oh, yes, Lieutenant. All of us physically and intellectually inferior females are fully capable of multiple acts of stupidity."

"Sarcasm is not worthy of a woman as obviously intelligent as you, Counselor. Thanks for your time, we'll let ourselves out."

"I hope I've been helpful."

"Perhaps more than you think."

April looked at me for a second time. A flashing glance. "Please close the door, Detective Paxton. I have work to do."

* * *

Agosto had noticed my chagrin over being treated like a fence post during the interview. "Don't let her get you down, Rock. Anytime a woman tries that hard to avoid looking at a guy, she's probably interested in him."

"You read that in the yellow pages, oh Master."

"No. Think it rubbed off on me in Psych 101."

"What about the weapon, Lieutenant?"

"Dollars to donuts…to use an original phrase…I believe that it's in Tampa."

12

The day following our interview with April, I got a call from the person with the Kazoo voice.

"Detective Paxton?"

"Yes?"

"I understand you're on the Davidson case."

"I'm an intern. Lieutenant Agosto is in charge."

"He isn't in. I guess you're it."

"Okay. What can I do for you?" By this time I was waving frantically for someone to pick up on my line.

"Having any luck, Detective?" The caller laughed. It

was as though a bee flew into my ear.

"Some. Do you have any information? A name?"

"You know who I am, Detective. Don't play games. I killed that pathetic creature Pete Davidson. And my name? Just call me Azrael. And so you won't have to look it up, it means *Angel of Death* or *Death's Bright Angel*. Appropriate don't you think? You may call me just plain Azrael if you like."

"Okay, Azrael. What can you tell me about the crime? Something that will convince me you're not just some nut trying to build a reputation."

"Some nut? Hardly. Okay, it went down this way. I had arranged to pick up Peter in front of the jewelry store. When he arrived…and was waiting for me…I called 911 from the booth across the street. When I saw the squad car coming, I placed two shots through the glass door to set off the alarm. I thought Pete would run and force you to shoot. But when he walked out with his hands up, I had no choice. A very nice shot, don't you think?"

"Effective," I said. "Anything else?"

"One other thing. After firing the shots, I looked for the shell casings, but I only found two. I guess you found the third."

"Okay, I believe you killed the man. Why?"

"Damn. You want me to solve your case for you? Just say I owed him big time. Maybe I just didn't like his looks.

Maybe he peed on my vegetable garden. Now…though I've enjoyed talking to you…It's time to say good-bye. Take care of yourself, Detective Paxton."

* * *

Agosto walked in five minutes or so after Azrael's call. Jim Klein whose desk was two in back of mine in the same row--saw Agosto and joined us grinning. "I saw you signaling, Rock. For a minute, thought you were trying to get permission to go potty."

"What's going on, Rock?"

"Got a call from Davidson's killer. Waved my hand trying to get someone to pick up. I guess Klein did."

"What'd you get, Jim?"

"Set up recording and a trace. Neither turned out well."

"Well you tried. Thanks," I said. Not wanting to appear stupid, I waited until Jim returned to his desk before I asked, "How'd he set up a trace and recording? I don't think he left his desk. Didn't have time."

"The marvelous age of super computers," Agosto said. He pulled out the typing leaf on my desk, and there in 16 point boldface type was the instruction sheet for initiating a recording and a trace. "I guess I forgot to tell you about our brand new super duper system. So much to learn, so little time to learn it, Rock."

"Jim's probably sitting back of me laughing his butt off."

"Probably. But he'll get over it. He's got butt to lose. So…what went down?"

I recounted the conversation with Azrael. After I finished, the Lieutenant said, "So we've got one of those… a teaser…a crack pot who wants to brag a little."

"Someone who thinks they're smarter than we are and is out to prove it?"

"You got it partner."

"And you think that person will kill again?"

"Most certainly."

"Probably keep killing 'til we get close…then go somewhere and give another division fits?"

"No…I don't think so, Rock. This baby had five people on a hit list. One down, four to go. When finished, he or she will disappear into the woodwork."

"You're still convinced it's all about the rape?"

"It's the only thing that makes sense. Another reasonable motive comes along, we'll take a look at it."

"And you believe April's suspect number one?"

"We're in no position to focus on one person. The only thing that really links anyone in the family is the weapon…and we can't be sure that it's the weapon used in the killing. If we're correct on the motive, it's April, her father…someone they hired…or some super citizen who thinks he or she is doing God's will."

"You still didn't mention me. I hate all those bastards."

"Like I told you…I checked you out good. All your friends had firm alibis."

"Alibis can be rigged."

"Nope. I can spot a phony alibi…like Rush Limbaugh says…with half my brain tied behind my back."

"One more question, Lieutenant?"

"Shoot."

"How do you tie up a brain?"

13

It was the day after Azrael's call and my day off. Nothing planned, I decided to visit April's mother. I don't know exactly why. Perhaps it was a desire to revisit a time when life was simpler. Of course, April was the bond that linked us. We both had loved her--still loved her--with a passion. And there was something else: April had been thinner then, but with maturation, her resemblance to her mother had become remarkable.

One thing was for damned sure. My inability to reconnect with April was more than a bother. It was a nagging drain on my sense of well being. Something was definitely missing in my life, and I knew what it was. Maybe my visit was a transference of sorts.

Whatever the reason, I had a need to talk to Maggie Perry. I arrived at the mansion, lifted the iron ring on the door, and let it drop. Its "clunk" echoed through the grand reception hall.

Dorothy, the same lady in gray answered the door. The same Dorothy, who had greeted me with a frown over eight years before. She looked much the same except the residual creases of her no nonsense scowl were deeper. Fixed with time.

"I'd like to speak with Ms. Perry, please."

"Mr. Paxton? Yes. Come in." She stepped away and I entered.

She left me standing there, and a few minutes later Maggie Perry appeared in the rear of the magnificent hall with its huge crystal chandeliers and stairway rising in a graceful curve to the second floor balcony.

"Rock. My God, it's been ages." The hug she gave me hurt way down. I needed such a hug, but not from her.

"Do you have a little time to talk, Ms. Perry?"

"Maggie, please. Of course." She took my hand and squeezed it before saying, "Come to my little work room, Rock. It's very comfortable …a nice place for conversation…and fun things."

She took my hand again and led me to her *little work room*. The room was twice the size of the *great* room in my condo: a desk, wall of bookcases, and a fireplace accompanied by enough natural tan leather furniture to handle several conversations simultaneously.

She led me to a couch and sat down. I picked a chair on the opposite side of the seating arrangement. She seemed disappointed.

Rock, it's so good to see you again. You certainly have matured into a very handsome young man," she stared at me until my face turned red. "April was very fortunate to have such a handsome…"

"Thanks, Maggie. You're very kind," I interrupted, "I may not be welcome when I tell you why I'm here."

"I think I know why," she said. "It's about that man who was shot…one of the bastards who raped April. I also know you're a detective now."

Bastards didn't sound quite right coming from her, but I shook it off and said, "Detective Intern actually…a new thing. I suppose Counselor Perry told you I was a police officer."

"Oh, yes. We keep each other informed about what's happening in our lives…we don't have many secrets… perhaps one or two." She giggled and her eyes measured me for a new suit.

"I didn't come to talk to you about Pete Davidson's murder, Maggie."

"Well…whatever the topic, it's good to see you. I get so lonely. Preston's away so much…in London now…for two more days." She sighed and smiled. It was a warm smile, and her eyes flirted. I was beginning to feel very uncomfortable. She was definitely trying to lead me into something. Something I definitely wanted to avoid, not being an adulterer by nature or inclination.

I recalled why I'd come and said, "I'd like to talk to you about April…not myself or the murder. You know how close April and I were, but now she won't even talk to me. Could you help me…give me some insight on how to get through to her. Help me break through that ice shell she's in?"

She pouted with her very kissable lips. "I thought perhaps that was the reason for your visit." She paused for a moment before saying, "Do you think I'm attractive, Rock?"

"Yes but…"

"And I think you're very handsome…so masculine. Such shoulders. I'll bet you're very, very strong." She ran the tip of her tongue over her lips.

It was going somewhere fast now. Too fast. I did the only thing I could do. I stood and prepared to defend myself. "Maggie, I shouldn't have come. It was a mistake."

"Mistake?" Her dreamy eyes flashed anger. Her kissable lips twisted as her face turned crimson. "You think I'm too old for you? I'm not…" A knock on the door stopped her.

The door opened and a guy so big that he made me feel like a leprechaun midget stood there. "Dorothy says it's time for your medication, Miz Perry." Maggie still pouted but seemed pacified by the sight of the big guy and the mention of her medication.

"Medication…yes. Thanks, dear." She looked at me and smiled, the anger gone, "I suppose it's time for you to leave, Rock. My medication makes me so sleepy. It's been so nice to see you again, dear. Stop by again…soon. We'll finish our little talk."

Dorothy came in and led her into the great hall and up the curving stairway. I was left face to face with the big guy. Actually, that isn't an accurate representation. His chin was even with the top of my head, and my eyes were focused on the second button of his open shirt.

"Why'd you bother Miz Perry?" His voice sounded like someone who'd taken a few shots to the throat. His nose was flat and crooked. More evidence that Tommy had done some time in the squared circle.

"A personal matter, Mister…"

"Tommy, punk. Tommy Purdue."

"Whatever you say, Tommy. You should know if anyone does." I stepped from under his shadow and out of the reach of his long muscular arms, reasoning he might not appreciate my burst of wit.

"No one discusses no personal matters with Miz Perry without the Counselor says so. You understand?"

"Of course."

"So what was so personal?" We exchanged steps. He took one toward me. I took one away from him, certain that he didn't want to tango.

Seeing an unpleasant situation shaping up, I whipped out my intern's badge and flashed it in his face. "Police business, Tommy. Now if you'll move, I'll be on my way."

Stymied, he stepped aside and said, "I'll have to report this to the Counselor, you know. He'll want to talk to you. Who should I say you was?"

"Tell him I was and still am, Rock Paxton."

"Rock," he snickered. "That's a kick. You look like a little pussy cat to me."

I felt like giving him a big meow, but was afraid he wouldn't laugh. Anyway, I'd given up doing animal imitations since the day--I was only ten at the time--I'd barked at the neighbor's terrier. The little sucker took exception to the taunt and nailed me on the ankle. When mom chided me for teasing, I used a form of the old standby excuse, "But, mom, he barked at me first."

14

The morning after my visit with Maggie Perry, the Lieutenant was in my face before I could sit. "Paxton. Come with me. Captain wants to see you."

I got up knowing that I was in for a chewing. No nice guy smile or punch in the arm. No, "Good to see you're still breathing, Rock." Fairly certain of the reason for the call from on high, and the Lieutenant's lack of interest in my well being, I followed him, hoping this was the time I would receive the slack suggested during my interview.

We followed the Captain's clerk who led us to his

office, cleared our entry, and held the door open for us. She closed the door and left us standing in front of the Captain's desk.

Captain Jackson didn't seem too disturbed. At least, he didn't look up and start screaming. He wasn't reading, signing papers, or scribbling a note. He sat silently staring at the fingers of his very large hands. After an extensive examination of his manicure, he took a pair of clippers from his middle desk drawer and nipped off a hangnail. After replacing the clippers, he looked up and said, "Sit." We sat without hesitation.

"Paxton...do you know the time difference between Tampa and London, England?"

"Approximately five hours...I believe."

"So if someone called Tampa from London...at say seven a.m. London Time...what time would it be here? Take your time, Paxton. I want you to be clear on this."

"Seven a.m. London time would be two a.m. here, Captain."

"Very good, Paxton. So if an irate citizen with a complaint would call the Major at seven o'clock, how do you think he'd react?"

"He'd...uh...be very angry."

"Damned angry, wouldn't you say?"

"Yes sir, damned angry."

"Now…suppose that damned angry Major would pick up the phone…following the London call…and call the head of Major Crimes…one Dewayne Jackson…how do you think said head of Major Crimes would feel? Take a guess."

"Very upset. Pissed."

"You got it, Rock. Right smack on the frigging button." The Captain gave Agosto a quick smile. Then he pinned me in my seat with his eyes and asked, "Why in the hell did you do it, Rock? Why?"

"It was personal, sir."

"Personal? You go to the residence of a hot shot attorney…who's a murder suspect…whose daughter is a murder suspect…whose whole damned family…may be…oh hell. Personal? What was this personal matter? I pray that it's reasonably rational."

"I wanted to talk to April's mother, Maggie Perry. I was stupid, sir."

"I don't disagree, but I'm probably irritable. Two thirty a.m. is little early for me. Did you know Ms. Perry is recovering from a nervous breakdown?"

"No sir."

"You didn't notice anything unusual about her behavior?"

"She seemed…uh…aggressive."

"Aggressive? In what way?"

"Well sir...I thought she was on the make."

"Okay, Rock. Don't go into detail."

"Thank you, sir."

"How did your visit end?"

"A very large dude named Tommy Perdue came in... told her it was time for her medication. Her maid took her away. Meek as a kitten. Then Perdue invited me to leave. Said he have to tell the Counselor about my visit. I left." I didn't mention the pussy cat thing. Comic relief didn't seem in order at the moment.

"Smart move." The captain shook his head and looked at his old friend and long time partner. "What do you think, Luis. Should we dump his butt back into a squad car...let Rich Martino baby sit him for a few years? Or should we cut him a little slack...long as he understands his little intern shield doesn't make him top dog in the department? Well?"

"Let me think about it, Captain."

"Lieutenant?"

"Yes?"

"For what it's worth, I'm damned sorry I let you and the Captain down...and I wouldn't blame you if..."

"Don't squirm. It's unbecoming...particularly for a guy named Rock."

The Lieutenant looked at the Captain and continued, "Let's keep him, Dewayne. He's got too much promise to throw back."

"Like I said, Luis, it's your call. I'll tell the Major your decision after he wakes up…and after I go home and get some sleep." He stood and walked by us. Standing at the door, he took his hat from a hall tree, and left Luis and me sitting in front of his empty desk.

PART THREE

Angelo Donato Meets Azrael

Revenge is kind of a wild justice….

Sir Francis Bacon - Essay: Of revenge

15

Angelo Donato stared belligerently at Josh Sampson. "Why the hell did you come here, Josh? You know damned well you're jeopardizing our paroles. I don't give a damn about you, but I'm not returning to Lawtey. I've got a girl, Donna...a good job..."

"Still a pussy, Angelo? You think your PO's got nothing better to do than spy on you?"

"Other people know I'm a parolee...like the guy I rent this place from. Some think we're perverts 'cause we got sent up on a rape charge."

"Raping a woman doesn't make you a pervert, Angelo. A kid's different. I've got no use for a guy who rapes kids."

"The Perry girl…she was a kid. Only sixteen. And there are folks like the Perrys…think we got off light."

"We got off light because the old man didn't want publicity …we did him a favor by keeping our mouths shut."

"That's all behind us, Josh. And I want it there. If the Perrys …or anyone else saw you come in…"

"If…If…If. You sound like a guy who spends his life worrying. What if your house burns down? What if your engine blows up? What if you slip and fall in front of a semi? Like they say, wake up and smell the perfume."

"Roses."

"What?"

"It's wake up and smell the roses."

"I know that. I was being original."

"Okay…you were being original. Now we've got that settled, I want you to leave. Like I said, you coming here was a bad move for both of us…if that makes me a pussy… I'm okay with it. That's better than another…"

"Okay, Angelo…I just stopped by to see if you'd heard about Pete Davidson." Josh walked toward the door.

"Yeah I heard a couple of months ago. Maybe three."

"That make you nervous?" Sampson smiled maliciously. He flexed his muscles and combed his long blond hair with his fingers.

"Why should that make me nervous?"

"Maybe it was a payback for raping the Perry girl."

"Payback? By who?"

"Maybe her jerk boyfriend, Rock Paxton. Maybe her old man or an ex-pug they got working for them…Tommy Perdue. Maybe her…she's back in town. The little stuck up bitch." Josh opened the screen door and stood on the small porch waiting for Angelo's response.

"Hell…it was over eight years ago. Why wait until now?"

"Some people have long memories. Got deep hate in them. I just felt that since you're a worrier, you might want to worry about that, Angelo baby. See you sometime."

"Don't bother. I'm not looking for trouble."

"Sure. But sometimes trouble comes looking for you. You just never know." The screen door slammed shut. Angelo didn't move immediately. When he did, he went directly to the inside door, closed and double locked it.

16

April left the elevator across the hall from her tenth floor condo. She entered the condo, locked and chained the door, and went directly to her bedroom. Standing next to a clothes hamper at the foot of her bed, she disrobed, dropping each article of clothing into the hamper as it was removed. Standing nude in the center of the room, she avoided looking at her reflection in the dressing table mirror across the room.

Looking at her nude body was a trigger that released the trauma of her humiliation by Josh Sampson and his quartet of hyenas. And despite the passage of time--which should moderate memories--she revisited the horror of having her clothing ripped and torn from her body. She experienced once again the piling on, the repeated penetration, and the mauling by the five panting, slobbering animals. Later they said only four actually raped her. **Only** four. She hadn't been counting.

In her dreams, she relived the shame of being found shivering, naked, and bruised in a vacant field, of being carried to the hospital in a musty blanket. And, of course, there was the careful examination, the touching, the wiping, the swabbing to remove the evidence left by the pack: saliva on her breasts, semen on and in her, matted blood in her hair, foreign hair combed from her pubic region. They'd been thorough. Very.

So it was, upon completing her shower, she donned a heavy robe before crossing in front of the bathroom mirrors. Leaving the bath, she went to the kitchen, made a salad, and poured a glass of milk. She took her meager fare to the condo's balcony and placed it on a wrought iron table for two. There had never been two at the table. Pulling up a chair, she sat facing Tampa Bay. Detached, she toyed with her salad, not seeing the glitter of a thousand lights moving around and across the bay and dancing on its dark surface.

Eventually, she finished her Spartan meal and returned to the kitchen. She rinsed her dishes and put them in the dishwasher. Following her normal routine, she went to the living room and sank into a soft leather recliner. She turned on her wall mounted plasma TV. The eleven o'clock news had just begun. The third story in the evening's coverage brought her upright and alert in her chair.

Rock Paxton was being interviewed by the female news anchor. A taped PR piece, they discussed Rock's assignment to a new intern program for detectives. Rock laughed about the redundancy of saying he was a guinea pig in a trial balloon.

April stared at the tanned, curly-haired man she adored at sixteen. His smile was still quick and infectious. His dark eyes laughed at and with the interviewer. At the mention of his football career and excellent qualifications for the intern program, he seemed embarrassed and responded only after prodding by the interviewer, who seemed titillated by his discomfort.

It was the same Rock, once the love of her young life. The same hard-nosed, dynamic running back she had cheered from the bleachers. Apparently--based on his behavior--he was the same gentle, deferential friend he'd been off the field--on the steps of the Perry Mansion, in his letters, and on the telephone. Tears filled her eyes as the interview ended, and the news was shifted to the male anchor reporting a murder in Gibsonton, a town south of Tampa peopled by carnival workers.

April found herself profoundly shaken by the short interview. She dried her eyes and tried to forget what she'd just seen and felt. Tried to forget what had cracked the icy façade that protected her from feeling anything that had to do with the male animal.

She eventually recovered from her emotional reaction to Rock's unexpected appearance in her living room. And anger replaced the feeling of regret, the need to see him.

"Damn those bastards. They won't allow me to forget… to live…to feel again. I won't have a man's rejection. His sympathy. What man could accept damaged goods? Admit it, kiddo, you desire Rock's companionship. But how long would he tolerate your resistance to touching, holding, kissing …love making? He wouldn't understand. Yeah, he'd pretend it didn't matter. He'd pity me. I don't want his pity. I want what we had. My innocence. His respect. Nothing could reclaim what those bastards took away. Prison time didn't pay for what those heathen bastards destroyed."

Her verbal rampage over, she went to a small breakfront and took out a bottle of vodka. She poured three fingers into a glass and added lime juice and ice. She returned to the balcony and searched the heavens for answers, for peace. There were no answers. There was no peace.

* * *

Shortly after midnight, I returned to my apartment. From an eight o'clock taping about the Detective Intern program, I'd gone to the alley to bowl in the department league. I smiled as I thought of the last ball I threw in the tenth frame. I'd rolled two strikes and needed seven pins to nail a win over Captain Jackson's team. I picked up nine, and we won the three game set by two pins.

When I congratulated the Captain for his final game of 265, he'd grunted and said, "Well…it wasn't good enough was it? I needed a 268 to beat your butts, didn't I?" I'd laughed at his response, which brought a quick scowl and warning from him, "Watch it, Rock. You're still on probation." I'd looked into his dark eyes and saw a smile, which carried away a brief moment of concern.

"Sorry, Captain. We'll take it easy on you next time."

"You'd better," he answered before slapping my back and walking away.

Still thinking about the post game banter, I dropped my ball bag into the foyer closet and went to the kitchen. Two ham sandwiches and a glass of milk later, I headed for the bedroom for a shower and six hours in the sack. I was down to my boxers when the telephone on the bedside stand rang. Trouble, I thought. What else for a cop after midnight?

"Brad Paxton here."

"You sure it's not…the Rock." A giggle followed the question.

"Look," I said, "I'm dead dog tired. What is it?"

"I called earlier…but you weren't there."

"Bowling night. Look, doll, is there a point to your call or are we just playing telephone footsie?"

"I saw you on TV tonight. You looked…good."

It hit me. "April. Is it you?"

"Have you forgotten my voice, Rock?"

"Never. I never could. But you sound a little strange, kid."

Another giggle. "Could be the vodka."

"What is it, April? A problem? Is there something I can do?"

"Problem? No. I jus' needed to hear your voice. Jus' wanted you to know there's…been no one else…since… you."

"April…I want to see you. Please, honey."

"No…don't think so…don't think it would work. Wanted to ask you to forgive me…for what happened… for the way I treated you…other day. Take care…Rock."

I wanted to tell her there was nothing to forgive. That I wanted to help her get over what had happened. But the line was dead and my revived hopes went dead with the disconnect. I sat on the edge of my bed shaking, wishing she were with me. But she wasn't and chances were slim she ever would be.

17

Preston Perry stared at the Lieutenant across an oval conference table located on one side of the Attorney's office suite. I hadn't said anything, so I was sort of out of the loop, which was okay, me being an unassuming intern and all.

"Are you accusing me of lying, Lieutenant?" Perry asked.

"Well…it could be construed as a lie, but for now we'll just call it a memory lapse."

"Okay. April says I purchased the 9mm Sig Sauer

handgun and gave it to her, contradicting my statement when you interviewed me. So what?"

"You admit you purchased and misplaced a semi-automatic of that caliber, which we had already verified from the dealer's records."

"So, if April says I gave her the weapon...I won't call her a liar."

"Somebody's not 'fessing up, Counselor."

"I really don't see the problem, Lieutenant. My memory is that I misplaced it. If she said I gave it to her, I probably did. And, as you said, I had a memory lapse."

"Interesting. She says you gave it to her for protection after she was raped...after she first denied knowing anything about such a weapon. What is it, Counselor? Was she lying before? Or is she lying now?"

Perry smiled and said, "Okay, Lieutenant. I gave the weapon to April. We both told a little white lie to protect each other. Does that satisfy you?"

"To a point. However, when I interview someone in a murder investigation, I don't expect 'little white lies' from people as conversant with the law as you and your daughter. Collusion to impede an investigation can't be taken lightly...as you know, sir."

"Okay. We screwed up. But face it, Lieutenant. The weapon that I purchased is probably not the one that killed the Davidson punk. And since you haven't found it...and probably won't…you have no way of determining whether or not it was."

"All right. Little white lies aside, you've admitted you didn't misplace the weapon…that you gave it to your daughter…I'm afraid the matter will continue to be a problem."

"In what way?"

"Your daughter said she forgot the weapon…left it behind in her apartment when she returned home."

"So?"

"We checked with the leasing agency, and they checked with the complex manager. Woman with an impeccable record…for over ten years. She recalls checking the apartment over with your daughter. On the record she keeps…for deposit purposes…she noted that the apartment was clean and no items were left behind by the lessee."

"She probably took the weapon."

"Don't think so. Miss Perry initialed the notation when her deposit was returned."

Preston Perry's face exchanged a golf course tan for a flamingo pink. He rose from his chair and began pointing and making sweeping gestures. "You're being petty, Lieutenant. And I resent it. First, unable to establish a reasonable motive for the crime, you're assuming that the murder was motivated by April's rape. A leap in logic supported by desperation. Second, you're assuming the weapon that I purchased was the murder weapon, something you can't prove. Third, you're taking an act…motivated by love between my daughter and me…to construct a ridiculous charge of attempted collusion designed to stymie your investigation. I see you as a very desperate investigator constructing a straw house that will topple with the first snort of the truth. You have nothing, Detective. But I'd be most happy to demonstrate that in court." A smug smile on Perry's face said it all. Case dismissed.

"Sure wish I'd have had you to defend me when I was ten and lifted two bananas from a fruit stand. Could have saved me from one good butt busting."

Perry wasn't amused. "Now…is there anything else? I'm very busy."

"For the record, Counselor, I still believe that the weapon in question was the murder weapon…but for Rock's sake, I hope it wasn't."

"As for your belief, Lieutenant, belief and truth are often miles apart."

"And sometimes, they sleep with each other… bedfellows, you know. One other thing, Sir."

"Yes?"

"We intend to interview your wife and your security man. Perdue."

"Like hell you will."

"At your home, here or downtown."

"Maggie's not well. I won't have you bothering her as Rock did. I won't permit it."

"It'll happen, Counselor. I know you can put up roadblocks...slow us down. But it will happen. Why make it difficult? You'll be present...with a doctor if you want. Think about it. I'll be in touch."

Luis stood but I stayed sitting. I had something to say. Staring into Perry's eyes, I said, "Counselor, the next time you have a beef about something I do, the Major, Captain Jackson and I would appreciate it if you'd wait 'til a reasonable hour to call. My superiors lost a lot of sleep and I took a good reaming. I was out of line...I'm sorry I bothered Maggie...and you were thoughtless." I was surprised by his response.

"The minute I hung up, I regretted making the call so early, Rock. Perhaps I shouldn't have called at all...but I love Maggie and April..." He stopped, shrugged, and extended a beefy hand.

"Sorry, man. I know you wouldn't deliberately hurt either of them. I hope your a-hole isn't too tender."

I accepted his firm handshake and comments with a modicum of suspicion. A cop thing...maybe. Was he angling for a pass? Looking for a friend in the ranks?

* * *

Angelo entered the Pizza Emporium at four p.m., his regular starting time. Waiting for him was the owner, Chick

Corelli, an ex-convict who employed ex-convicts. Chick had been an entrepreneur dealing in marijuana before being sent up. He'd stashed a quarter of a million in cash before being caught. Now, ten years after his release, he was a pizza store and real-estate entrepreneur, owning seven of the former and several new properties in Ybor City.

An old-town section bordering downtown Tampa, Ybor city had once been a flourishing cigar manufacturing enclave. Now, it was being rapidly redeveloped into an attractive and active entertainment, business and residential site.

Chick liked Angelo Donato for several reasons. First, there was the matter of the Italian heritage. Then, there was the height factor. Both short --five four max--standing face to face, they could touch noses. Third, after the first year of employment, Angelo had earned Corelli's respect as a hard-working, punctual, and honest young man. So it was that Corelli awarded him by making him manager of Pizza Emporium - No 1. To Corelli, all employees were treated with utmost respect--unless they proved they weren't worthy of respect. He called males "my man" and females "my lady".

Across the street from the *Pizza emporium - No 1*, Azrael sat in a rental car with tinted windows and watched the camaraderie between the friends. The chubby one patting the slender one on the back, joking and laughing with him. Smiling, Azrael muttered, "Sorry, chubs, you're going to require a new manager very, very soon."

18

At nine a.m. Angelo Donato entered Chick Corelli's office in Ybor City. Chick was at his desk working over a stack of invoices. He glanced up at his employee and young friend. His man. What he saw on Angelo's face told a story. Something was wrong.

"Sit, my man. Remember my slogan. You got a problem, Chickaroo's here for you." After shaking Chick's hand, Angelo dropped heavily into a desk side chair. He laid a folded sheet of paper on the stack of invoices and sighed.

"Yeah, Mister Corelli, I think I got a problem. A big problem."

"Corelli took a sip of coffee before unfolding and reading the brief note that Angelo found so disturbing. It was an unusual, computer-generated type face, which contributed to its malevolent message:

ANGELO BABY, YOU SLEEPING WELL THESE DAYS? SOMETIMES PEOPLE DIE IN THEIR SLEEP YOU KNOW. SOME WITH BULLET HOLES IN THEIR HEADS. SOME WITH KNIVES IN THEIR CHESTS. SOME WITH NEEDLES IN THEIR ARMS. OH SO MANY WAYS TO DIE. DISTRESSING, DON'T YOU THINK? BUT, DAMN, EVERYONE DIES EVENTUALLY. I SUGGEST YOU START PREPARING FOR THE BIG SLEEP. MAYBE THE PLUMP LITTLE PIZZA MAN WILL PROTECT YOUR BACK WHILE YOU PREPARE FOR THE INEVITABLE. LOOK AROUND. I'LL BE THERE SOMEWHERE...WAITING... WAITING...WAITING.

AZRAEL - THE ANGEL OF DEATH

"Where was this, Angelo? Where'd you find it?"

"Under my wiper blade this morning. Went out of the house 'bout seven thirty...going to Donna's place...and it was there. Someone's going to kill me, boss. I know it...same person who killed Pete. And I think I know who it is, I think."

"Double 'I think', my man, which means you're far from certain. Maybe it's a kid trying to be funny...in a weird way. A jokester getting his morning kick. There are a lot of weirdos out there. Each with his own thing."

"I think it's a guy I went to school with. Guy who planned the rape of the Perry girl. Josh Sampson."

"And why would this Sampson character want to kill you?"

"I don't know. Maybe because I...we ratted on him for a deal. He got the longest sentence...didn't serve the minimum, though."

"Has he threatened you?"

"Came to see me the other day...Tuesday. Started putting me on about being such a pussy for worrying about us being seen together...said maybe I should worry about what happened to Pete Davidson...'stead of worrying about whether the PO was going to find us together. Said someone connected to the Perry girl might be out to get the guys who did the rape...like Pete. Said maybe it was a revenge hit."

"Sounds as though he was hypothesizing, not threatening you."

"So, maybe he's right about the other...the Perry family...maybe someone they got under contract to hit us."

"Seems odd, my man. Why wait eight years to start getting revenge?"

"Hell...I don't know what to think. You're right, Mister Corelli. If it's the family, why would they wait? I know one thing for damned sure."

"What's that?"

"That note's creepy. It scares the hell out of me."

"Well, my man, there's only one thing we can do about that note." Corelli rose from his chair, refolded the note and put it in an inside jacket pocket.

"What's that, boss? One thing to do?"

"Take this ugly piece of crap to the detective who's handling the Davidson case...Lieutenant Agosto...I think it is. See if he knows anything about this Azrael dude. And see if we can get you some protection until they put the sick bastard on ice."

* * *

I turned off the tape deck and returned my copy of the case file to its place in my file drawer. For the third time that morning, I had reviewed all the reports and recorded and handwritten interview notes that had been made so far during the Davidson investigation: Recorded interviews with Davidson's PO, friends, family and employer; recordings of the 911 call, medical examiner's report, and crime scene interviews. A whole lot of stuff that amounted to a whole lot of nothing. Ditto, copies of notes taken during interviews with April and her father and the remaining four punks involved in the rape.

A review of the forensic evidence--again--was as futile as fishing for brown trout on the Mississippi delta: one shell casing and three slugs--one from Davidson's chest and two from inside the jewelry store; two hundred sets of mostly smudged prints from the phone booth and no matches of note. Put all together what we had didn't amount to diddly squat on toast.

Sheila Adams--the cute receptionist--broke through my exercise in futility. She leaned on my desk and said, "Two little guys out front say they need to speak with the person working on the Davidson case. The Lieutenant's not available, so I guess you're up, Rock."

"Okay, Sheila. Send them in please."

"Right." She batted her bright blue eyes and flashed her very white teeth. Nice eyes, nice teeth, and--since mom may read this--her physical arrangement was exceptionally well displayed as she walked away.

A minute later, Sheila returned leading two very short Italian types. One, I recognized immediately as Angelo Donato. At the sight of Donato, my temperature eased up a notch or two.

"Take a seat, men. Sorry Lieutenant Agosto's not available." They settled into the hard wooden chairs, and I said, "Introduce your friend, Donato." I couldn't resist biting off the words. Curt, I suppose you'd call it.

Angelo responded to my request. "This is my boss, Mister Chick Corelli. Mister Corelli owns seven pizza stores...Pizza Emporiums...and a lot of property over in Ybor city."

"How interesting. How's the pizza business, Corelli?" Looking at Angelo, I was dealing with a lot of anger. Corelli picked up on it.

"I sense some animosity on your part, Paxton."

"Do you?"

"I do. You get as angry as you damned well please when we're done. I understand the attitude, but we didn't come here so you could blow off about something that happened over eight years ago. So quit being a hard ass and listen up. You could learn something."

I couldn't avoid a smile. Corelli was a tough little guy. He'd been around. "Sorry, Mister Corelli. I'll curb the attitude. What's the problem?"

"The problem is this, Detective." he reached into his jacket and pulled out Azrael's note. He leaned back and watched my face as I read the taunting death threat. I don't know what he saw, but I know what I felt. As I put the message down, one important thing had happened: I no longer doubted the motive for the murder of Pete Davidson. The rape was the motive. And the five rapists were the targets of this Azrael, whoever he...or she...was. And I realized someone I loved could be a sadistic murderer.

19

I had just finished recording the interview with Angelo Donato when the Lieutenant arrived and introduced himself. I explained the nature of Angelo's concerns, said I'd taped the interview, and asked if he'd like to hear the recording. He said he would, and I played it.

The Lieutenant was silent for a moment. When he started talking, I was pleased by his first remark and learned a lot from the commentary that followed. "Good interview, Rock. Angelo, we're going to give you as much protection as it takes. If we do it correctly, we could take this maniac down. This threat, I believe, seals the deal as far as the motive for Davidson's murder is concerned…" he paused to look at me. I nodded in agreement and he continued, "We can be reasonably certain that the rape of April Perry is the motive for his murder and this threat on your life."

"This Azrael nut probably knows that you're here… or suspects that you'd come here when you got the note. And he or she probably knows your daily routine from bacon to bedtime. So we're going to ask you to change that routine…"

"But I have to go to work." Angelo broke in. He glanced at his watch, a gift from his girl, Donna Infante. "I've got to be there at four…in six hours."

"No you don't, my man. I'll take over for you," Corelli said and patted Angelo's arm.

Agosto continued. "Until I talk to the Captain and get approval for twenty four hour protection, I want you to stay home. Detective Paxton will take you there and stay with you…until I arrange for someone else to take over."

Agosto was percolating. He turned his attention to me. "Rock, you will check all the doors and windows and pull down all the blinds…"

"They're verticals. All of my blinds are verticals," Angelo said with a touch of pride.

"Verticals. Right. Rock you will assist Angelo in closing his verticals. In addition, you'll identify a place in the house where he can safely turn on a light after dark…"

"Spare bedroom don't have any windows, Lieutenant."

"Good, Angelo. The spare bedroom it is. After you leave, I'll direct the 911 operators to treat any call from you as a priority. Do you have a redial feature on your telephone?"

"Yes sir. On my cell phone."

"Good. Paxton, dial 911 before you leave Angelo's place. Tell the operator you're setting up a redial for Angelo Donato…they'll know what it's all about. And Angelo, if you hear anything unusual…the slightest sound…hit that redial button and just say 'Donato' when the operator responds. Okay?"

Corelli spoke up. "I'm willing to sit with Angelo tonight."

"Thanks but no thanks, Corelli. We've got a chance to nail this mutant. Having another civilian on site could complicate matters. You understand?"

"Got it, Lieutenant. Thanks for your help. Angelo's a good kid, an opinion not shared by Detective Paxton, I'm afraid. But that's forgivable, I suppose…seeing as how… well…no hard feelings detective?" Corelli leaned over my desk and stuck out his right hand. I accepted it without reluctance. Angelo didn't bother to seek reconciliation.

* * *

Angelo's home was small: Two bedrooms, bath, living room, kitchen with a six by six dining area. There was a small porch off the kitchen. Sitting on one side were an automatic washer and dryer, neither in top shape.

Angelo and I followed the Lieutenant's instructions step by step. Windows checked and locked. In the case of one lower window panel with a broken lock, I drove several finishing nails into the frame of the upper panel fastening each panel in place. We closed the vertical blinds, which were in surprisingly good condition. Angelo said he got them on sale at Sears, a bargain he couldn't refuse. I said, "How nice."

At dark, I did a security check outside. Nothing going on except the chirping of tree frogs positioned to take down a few bugs. Returning to the house, I helped Angelo move a console TV into the bedroom without windows. When that was done, I called 911, setting up the redial.

Once again, I explained what he had to do after I left. "One noise you can't explain, you hit the redial button." He responded with a nod.

He left the bedroom and went to the kitchen and returned carrying three cans of Miller Light.

Before I could decline an offer to have a beer--for the first time since we'd left the station--he looked directly into my eyes and said, "I got these for myself...thinking you wouldn't drink with a man who did what I did. I want you to know I hate what I did, and I don't expect you to forgive me. I wouldn't."

I was going to say, "You got that right." I changed my mind, thinking it was time for me to cut him a little slack. Maybe.

* * *

At eleven thirty I was watching the Florida Sports channel. Angelo was stretched out on the bed, making like a schnauzer with a sinus problem. My cell phone rang and it was Agosto.

"You still awake?" he asked.

"Barely. What's up?"

"We have you covered. There's an unmarked car outside. Go get some shuteye, Rock...and make an outside check before you leave. Hey...what in the hell's that noise?"

I held the telephone over Angelo's face. "That, Lieutenant, is the mating sound of an Angelotus Donatus primed by three cans of Miller Lite."

"Go home, Rock. It may be catching. Angelotus Donatos, wise guy." Agosto hung up laughing. And I retired from my nocturnal watch after checking with the detectives in the unmarked vehicle.

20

The clock radio on Donna Infante's nightstand buzzed. And the tiny woman's eyes opened slowly. She resisted an urge to turn "the damned thing" off and swung her short but shapely legs over the side of the bed. She had to scoot forward to touch the floor with her size five feet.

Donna was a five foot one inch nymph with bright blue eyes and curly brown hair. A button nose that wrinkled when she laughed turned her oval face into that of a child riding a Ferris wheel.

During the year she and Angelo had being going

together--they'd met at a church festival--Donna had risen at six a.m. so she could shower, dress and have breakfast ready by seven-thirty. That's when Angelo would come through the door, ready to eat, to laugh at little things, to hold her hand, and to share a kiss or two until she left for work at eight-forty-five.

Donna exited her shower, dried, and put on bra and panties. After slipping into a flowered silk dressing gown, she went to kitchen and turned on the automatic coffee maker. From there, it was out the front door to retrieve the newspaper, which would be right where the front sidewalk crossed her driveway. She reached the spot. It wasn't there.

Donna looked around. Her front lawn. Her neighbor's lawn. The street. Finally, she turned toward the rear of the house. Her paper lay in front of the garage doors, fifty feet away. "Andrew must have eaten his Wheaties this morning," she said. The reference was to a sixty year old retiree who earned a little money and got his exercise delivering the *Tampa Tribune*.

The moment Donna disappeared from view, a shadow separated itself from the shade between the house and a large shrub beside the front steps. Azrael easily made it up the steps and into the house before Donna returned. Smiling, pleased with the ruse, the dark visitor waited in the foyer behind the open front door.

Donna entered the foyer and turned to close the door. Reading the lead of the featured story, she didn't see the arc of the arm or the gloved hand holding the 9mm semi-automatic pistol that slammed into the side of her skull. She sank to the floor unconscious and didn't see the smiling face of her attacker bending down to check her pulse. Azrael was pleased to find a strong heart beat. Killing her wasn't a part of the plan. Because Donna was such a tiny person, Azrael had no difficulty dragging her into a small bedroom at the rear of the house. Taping her mouth and hands, placing her in a small closet, and jamming a chair back under the door knob completed the first part of the task. The second part would be more satisfying. And much easier.

Returning to the living room, Azrael picked up the newspaper, dragged a chair to the middle of the living room, turned it to face the foyer, and sat down to wait.

* * *

At seven-thirty a.m., I was on my way to work and felt a need to check on Angelo. I dialed his number and waited. After the tenth ring, I decided something was wrong. Calling dispatch, I was told that a patrol car had reported all was okay on the last pass at seven fifteen. I asked the operator to contract the unit and request a meet me at the residence ASAP.

I arrived and found the patrol car and two uniformed officers waiting in the driveway. I wheeled in behind them.

I showed my badge and said, "Detective Intern Paxton. I called the subject and got no answer."

"We don't think anything's happened to him, Detective."

"Why not?"

"His car was in the driveway at seven ten. Gone now."

"Your names?"

"Corporal Dan Patitsas and Officer George Ihnat."

"I have a key. Let's check out the house to make certain."

A quick check inside was negative. No sign of Angelo. No evidence of a brawl or break in. I called Agosto and explained the situation. His response was quick and unkind.

"I told the little bastard to stay in his house."

"Obviously, he didn't take you seriously."

"Obviously. You say he left the house between seven fifteen and seven thirty?"

"That's what Corporal Patitsas says."

"Where in the hell…I'll try to get in touch with Corelli. See if he's got any ideas."

We left the house. I got into my car and headed to Central after asking the two uniforms to hang out in case Angelo returned. And to call Lieutenant Agosto if he did

* * *

As expected, Angelo reached Donna's house at seven thirty. In his rush to see her, he stumbled and fell on the steps. He got up laughing. He'd tell Donna he'd fallen for her again. Opening the door, he called her name. After closing the door, he walked from the foyer and faced his worst and final nightmare. The killer's lips moved. "Good morning, Angelo. Good bye, Angelo."

"Oh, no…why…please don't. Please…" The muzzle spit flame, and a single slug smacked into Angelo's forehead, driving him backward into the foyer. Azrael checked Angelo's condition, careful not to step in the pool of blood forming around the victim's head. When satisfied that the mission was over, the weapon and gloves went into a back pack that matched Azrael's jogging outfit, a navy blue silk blend. The cold-faced killer went through Donna's attached garage and entered her rear yard. Once there, it was simple matter to follow a six foot hedge into an abutting lot and end up one street over from the one fronting Donna's property. Jogging easily on the sidewalk, it was only a two block run to where Azrael had parked a pewter Chrysler 300. Within fifteen minutes, the backpack, it's contents and the jogging outfit were in a locker at a private health club. Azrael had showered away the acrid odor of gunpowder, dressed and left the club feeling very pleased.

21

At ten a.m., Hugh Offerman left his office at the Second National Bank, Temple Terrace Branch. Hugh was distraught. One of his prize employees had failed to show for work. Hadn't called in. As manager of the branch, he would have to put her on notice. A very difficult task because she had been such an outstanding employee, and he was--well--very fond of her.

He drove into her driveway, opened the car door, slid from the seat, and walked up the steps. He prepared to knock on the door, but paused to straighten his navy blue tie that went so well with his navy blue suit and his navy blue socks. To say he was a conservative dresser would be akin to saying a wounded tiger was unfriendly. Finally prepared, he knocked on the door. It opened. Leaning forward, he asked, "Donna, may I come in? It's Hugh… Mister Offerman." No response. He'd have to be more forceful. He pushed the door and it bumped into an object on the floor. He pushed harder, and it opened enough for him to slide through. He stared at the obstacle blocking the door and felt his legs grow weak.

"Oh my God…goodness. Oh…Donna are you here? Are you all right? Oh God in Heaven." He fumbled a cell phone from his jacket pocket and urged a trembling index finger over three numbers. 9--1--1.

* * *

I was in the reception area gabbing with Sheila. The Lieutenant came through the door from the squad room. His face told me he had bad news.

"What is it, Lieutenant?"

"The bastard got to Donato."

"Damn. Where?"

"His girl friend's house…in Temple Terrace."

"So that's where he went. Not to speak ill of the dead, but he was…"

"Stupid." Agosto interrupted and said what I had hesitated saying. He continued, "I called Corelli all morning and couldn't connect. He finally returned my calls…five minutes after the murder was reported by the girl's boss. To top it off, the Pizza man knew the girl's address. If I'd made the connection earlier, we might have saved Angelo's butt."

"What time was the hit?"

"Don't know yet. The crime scene unit and the ME are already on the way. Let's get humping. The Medical Examiner…Milton Bosch…is an ex-detective. He just loves to put on his Sherlock Holmes cap and relive the past."

On the way to the crime scene, Agosto continued to tell me stories about Bosch. "One night, Milt got shot in the neck by a punk who'd killed a shop owner. Guy was hiding at the scene when Bosch and I got there. I shot the bastard when Milt went down."

"You were Bosch's partner?"

"Yeah…until he had enough and went to medical school."

"That when you teamed up with the Captain?"

"Yeah. Twenty five years ago."

"Damn, you must have been young."

"Yeah. I was a smart assed young punk like…"

"Your new partner?"

"Something like that." We wheeled to the curb behind the crime scene van and walked toward the house. We ducked beneath the yellow crime scene tape and approached one of the uniformed officers who had been on the scene that morning.

"Hello again, George," I said. "Still around?"

"Like the mail man…come rain, snow, hail and all that crap."

"Your buddy around back?"

"Was last I looked. Unless he sneaked into the garage to smoke a little pot. Kidding."

"Right." We entered the house, stepping around Angelo's body. A sturdy man with a shock of brown hair was kneeling beside the corpse. Doctor Milton Bosch was of average height and well constructed. Muscular, size seventeen neck--with a scar---broad shoulders, and a slim waist suggestive of an ex-jock or someone whose hobby was pumping iron. His shock of brown hair was too brown and didn't match his multi-hued goatee. He stood and shook Agosto's hand.

"What's the story, Milt?"

"We've got a solid time of death. Seven thirty…based on what the girl says." He pointed to Donna Infante who was sitting on a couch with a tall, thin guy's arm draped over her shoulders. Both had very long faces. The guy's was natural, hers the result of sudden sorrow. "Guy with her is her boss…manages a branch bank on Fiftieth street.

Name's Offerman…Hugh Offerman. Girl's…Donna Infante."

"God. She looks like a kid. A pretty kid," I said.

"Yeah…closer you get, the prettier she gets. Tiny thing."

"You about done here?" Agosto asked. A flash went off and we stepped aside to avoid appearing in the crime scene photos.

"Give Agnes another ten minutes," Bosch said. He pointed at the chair facing the foyer. "The angle of the wound…looks as though the shooter was sitting in that chair and popped Donato when he turned around from closing the door. Body got moved some when Offerman forced his way in. He says a few inches. Drag mark in blood--from Donato's head--says it was closer to a foot."

"You got the perp's name?" Agosto asked.

"Give me a couple hours, for heaven's sake."

Startled at the exchange, I glanced at their faces. They were smiling like a couple of Barbary apes.

"You playing poker this Saturday night, Milt?"

"Probably. Have to look around and see if I have anything left from last Saturday."

"Dust off a few hundred. I could use it. Youngest kid's in college, you know."

"Don't tell me your problems. Now…why don't you get the hell out of the way and talk to the girl…and her boss?

Keep you occupied. You need any tips on interviewing, give a whistle."

They shook hands. Mutual affection was written on their faces. We crossed the living room to where Donna Infante and Offerman waited. On the way, Agosto stopped and picked up a leather Ottoman. He put it on the floor in front of Donna. He sat facing her, reached out and took one of her hands and held it between both of his. The arrival of another source of sympathy caused Offerman to remove his arm from around her shoulders.

"I'm Lieutenant Agosto. The guy with the curly hair is my partner, Rock Paxton. How ya' doing, kid? You up to telling us about this bad situation?"

"Yes sir," she sniffled, "I'll do anything...if it helps get the madman who killed Angelo."

"Good girl. Now, just take us through what happened. Take your time and try to remember the details. Detective Paxton will be recording our conversation if it's okay with you and Mister...Offerman."

Both nodded. Donna began. She told us about Angelo's daily visit for breakfast then proceeded through the morning's events. She finished with a recap of how she found her newspaper misplaced. And when she returned with the paper and stepped into the foyer, she'd been slugged in the head. And she awoke in the closet with her ankles and wrists taped together and her mouth taped shut. Then it was Offerman's turn.

"When Donna didn't report off, I was concerned. I decided to check on her. I came here and found the door open. I called for Donna, but there wasn't any answer, which increased my concern. I pushed on the door and found it blocked. I pushed harder and the obstacle moved enough for me to enter. I found the obstacle was…uh… Angelo's body. Of course, I was shocked and feared for Donna's safety. I pulled myself together and called 911. I heard a banging from the spare bedroom. I went in the room, found that the noise was coming from the closet. I removed a chair blocking the door and found Donna bound as she described. I removed the duct tape and got her a glass of water. Put the tape used to bind her on the bed along with the roll from which it came. That's it."

Agosto looked at me and nodded. I turned off the recorder. "Very well done, guys. Now, I'm going to give you my card, and if anything comes to mind…any little detail…a voice sound…a cough. Anything. You call." The Lieutenant turned to Offerman, "I'm just a cop, sir. But if I were you…and I know how heavy your responsibilities must be…but I'd suggest that you give Miss Infante some time off with pay…you know…a week or two."

"Certainly, Lieutenant. I believe Donna has vacation time coming…even if I…uh…couldn't get approval for the other…but I will try."

"Good man. And Donna, do you have family or a friend you could stay with…until your place gets cleaned up?"

"My mother lives in Orlando. I could go there."

"Good. I'm going to ask Detective Paxton to help you around here until you're ready to go…packed and everything. Then, if you don't mind, I'd really appreciate it if you'd drop him off downtown before you leave for Orlando."

I looked at her and she looked at me. I didn't mind a bit and she didn't seem to. Only Offerman seemed put off by the arrangement.

I walked outside with Agosto. "You match making, Lieutenant?"

"Pretty single girls like Donna should be comforted by single guys…not by married dudes like Offerman. Did you notice his wedding ring?"

"No."

"I think we may have saved him from a lifetime of regret."

"You seem chipper…considering."

"Not chipper. Grateful . Grateful for one thing only."

"What's that?"

"Angelo was dead at seven thirty…just about the time we missed him. He blew it. We didn't. Azrael knew exactly where and how to get him. Smart bastard. Knew more than we did about the target' s habits.

22

For the three days following Angelo Donato's murder, the Lieutenant and I and six detectives on loan from other units canvassed the area for four blocks in all directions from Donna's home. The results were meager: One neighbor thought he heard a shot at seven-thirty. He went outside, saw nothing unusual, and returned inside. A Publix employee saw a pewter-colored vehicle leave the parking lot around seven-forty-five. The vehicle's windows were tinted. She couldn't see the occupant.

We were in the Lieutenant's office with Milton Bosch.

He had brought the autopsy and crime scene unit reports. The slug that killed Donato was not from the weapon that killed Davidson. Donna was a very neat housekeeper. There weren't many usable fingerprints. Donna's and Angelo's and three other sets had been identified: Offerman's and two of Donna's female friends from work. One three-inch strand of black hair had been found on the chair from which the killer had fired the fatal shot. No root. A mitochondria DNA match was a possibility. Outside, a navy blue cotton blend thread had been found on the shrub beside the front steps. Other than that, nada.

So, lumped together, the evidence available from the two murder scenes and the two corpses proved one thing. Azrael was cautious and clever. I said something like that and drew a response from Agosto.

"Yeah, perp's that and more, Rock. But one thing we know. These murders aren't over. And between now and the next one, we've got to out think this beast from Hell. They all make mistakes. This one will."

"Seems like the biggest problem will be determining which of the remaining three will be next on the hit parade," Bosch said. "And I doubt if you can dig up the manpower to protect all three twenty-four seven."

"I've thought about that, Lieutenant."

"Shoot, Rock."

"Why not put them all together in a safe house? Two men could baby sit them at night…might be all we'd need since they all work days. We could escort them to and from work. Probably wouldn't try to take down three guys in daylight."

"One problem with your thinking, Rock."

"What's that?" I controlled my chagrin over Agosto's comment.

"The word 'probably' suggests a window of opportunity we'd have to close. But I like the safe house thing. How about it, Milt?"

"Kid's bright."

Agosto looked at me and smiled. "Let's get together with the Captain and go over the possibilities and the resources. I've got an appointment with the big guy in ten minutes. Hate to leave you, Milt. You want an escort back to your tomb?"

* * *

Four weeks had passed since Donato's murder. Three months since Davidson's. Little progress had been made in either case. We had convinced two of the remaining three targets to stay in a safe house located in Seffner, a Tampa suburb. Frank Panteras and Misha Pulaski accepted the offer.

Josh Sampson declined, saying that if the bastard came after him, he'd break his or her frigging neck. We checked his house. He had a security system and more locks than the Main River.

So that's where it stood. Three months after the first of Azrael's crimes, two detectives were doing night duty with Panteras and Pulaski. And two others were assigned to escort them to and from work. Panteras worked in a machine shop with ten other men and two women. Pulaski was employed in a small slaughter house. Only four others worked there, but the manager held a gun permit and said he'd use it "anyone messes with Misha" whom he said was an excellent worker.

One other thing of note. Two weeks after Angelo's death, Donna Infante returned home. In the neighborhood one Saturday afternoon, I decided to stop by and see how she was doing. Kid probably needed cheering, I thought. Maybe I was the one who needed cheering. I knocked on her door. Had to knock a second time before she opened the door and stood there flushed and out of breath. She was wearing shorts and a T-shirt.

"Oh…it's you, Detective Paxton."

"It sure is. You been running from someone?"

She reached to her curly brown hair, "I must look like a witch. I was working out on my treadmill…oh, excuse me, please come in…if you're not afraid I'll bake you in my oven…"

"You look great, kid. And…please…call me Rock." She stepped aside and I went in. I noticed several changes. There was a new rug in the foyer. The infamous chair-- the chair from which Azrael had fired the fatal shot--was gone.

"I've got some fresh ice tea…would you like some?" she said.

"If you're drinking, I won't let you drink alone. Bad manners, you know."

Well, that's the way it started. After I left Donna, I found myself thinking what a great kid she was. Then, I decided that she wasn't a kid, but a very attractive woman.

PART FOUR

*Three frightened rapists all in a row,
which of the three will be next to go?*

Whoever fights monsters should see to it that
in the Process he {she} does not become one.

Nietzsche - Beyond Good and Evil

23

Finishing his lunch, Frankie Panteras did a "no no" and lit up a cigarette. His brand new wife Mattie had made breaking him of his "filthy habit" her number one wifely duty in his re-education as a husband. He didn't quite understand why this had become so important, since it had never come up while they were dating.

Now that he was spending nights away from home, he was willing to take a chance she wouldn't detect the odor on his clothes when he made visits home escorted by a detective. A deal had been struck. When he finished work at five o'clock--his regular quitting time--his escort would take him home to spend a couple of hours with Mattie. If he had to work overtime, the trip to their remodeled house in North Tampa was off limits. It was felt that darkness was Azrael's ally, despite the fact that Angelo had been killed in the morning. That had been his fault.

As he puffed away, his thoughts traveled a devious path: He wasn't working overtime, so he'd be visiting Mattie this afternoon, and so he'd ask his escort to stop so he could buy some breath mints and maybe some spray deodorize for his clothes. Working in a machine shop had a benefit in terms of his plan for deceiving Mattie. Lava soap was available in the washrooms. It was essential to the removal of soil from his hands after work. It was also great for removing nicotine stains from his middle and index fingers after a smoking binge.

Frankie finished his smoke and snubbed it out. He started back to his lathes and met his boss half way.

"Hey, Frankie. This letter came for you yesterday... forgot to give it to you."

"Thanks, Mister Bloom. Wonder who'd write to me here?" He ripped open the envelope and read the message. His face turned white. "Damn bastard. Knows where I work. Probably knows where I'm staying."

"Here. Let me look at that," Bloom said and removed the note from Frankie's limp fingers.

HEY, FRANKIE. YOU MISSING YOUR FELLOW RAPISTS? BET YOU ARE. AND I'LL BET YOU'RE WONDERING WHO WILL BE NEXT. YOU, MISHA, OR JOSH? SOMEONE HAS TO BE FIRST. YOU WANT TO VOLUNTEER? YOU KNOW, GET IT OVER WITH. NO USE POSTPONING THE INEVITABLE. I'LL BE IN TOUCH. OH, YOU MIGHT WANT TO GET SOME POLICE PROTECTION FOR YOUR PRETTY LITTLE WIFE. THERE'S MORE THAN ONE WAY TO REPAY A DEBT. SEE YOU FOR SURE. VERY SOON.

AZRAEL, ANGEL OF DEATH

"This is one mean sicko. What time's your escort due?" Bloom asked.

"Five o'clock. Unless I call and tell him I have to work over."

"Come to the office. We're going to call him early."

* * *

On IS-75, Azrael was returning to Tampa from Ocala in a blue Malibu that had been exchanged for a pewter Chrysler 300. The smug killer had cooled the rental agent's curiosity by saying the Chrysler's gas mileage left much to be desired.

Azrael plotted while driving--wondering now if Frank Panteras had gotten the note. The note was intended to divert the focus of his protectors. The mention of Frank's wife, was designed to spread the police resources. But Misha would die first.

Azrael had systematically tracked Misha and Frank and their escorts for several days, breaking off the tail occasionally to prevent being detected.

Azrael knew where the safe house was and knew the behaviors of the protectors and the protectees. Knew when and how an unexpected breakdown in the protection would occur, and knew exactly when Misha--the butcher--would be butchered.. Some humor there. Not much, just some.

* * *

We all got together in the Captain's office. I was standing by the door due to a shortage of chairs and my late arrival. The others present were the Captain, Agosto, Panteras and his boss--Bloom--the two detectives assigned to the safe house at night, and the two who escorted Panteras and Pulaski to and from the safe house. We all had copies of Azrael's latest note.

After a visual check of the attendance, Captain Jackson said, "This bastard--or bitch--isn't going to let up. Which means we have to be better prepared and better informed than we were in the Donato situation. By threatening one of the three remaining rapists--and his wife--Azrael may be using a magician's ploy…you know…causing an audience to watch one hand while doing something devious with the other. What do you think of that possibility, Lieutenant?"

"Very possible. Perhaps probable. Wants us to concentrate on protecting Frank while the bullseye is on Pulaski's back. Maybe Sampson's."

"What's your take, Rock?"

"I'll go with the Lieutenant's 'probable'. The s.o.b.'s clever...and perhaps cocky. Two successful hits. Both under our noses. Why not try to decoy us?"

"Any suggestions for coverage? Please don't everyone talk at once," Jackson said, his dark eyes sweeping the group. A hand went up. "You have the floor, Klein."

"Why not make it appear like we're doubling up on Frank? Two of us escort Frank home and stay there. Put the same two guys inside the safe house with Pulaski. But put two additional detectives outside."

"Okay. Well...we've got two for Frank and his wife's escort and protection. We've got the same two men for inside with Pulaski. So who do we have for the outside stake out?" Jackson's eyes settled on Agosto then pinned me to the wall.

"Rock and I will do the stake out, Captain. Right, Rock?"

"You bet, Lieutenant. What about Sampson?"

"Screw Sampson. He seems to believe he can protect himself. We'll tell him what's up and wish him luck."

"Just a thought, Sir," I said.

"Okay. Now let's talk about procedures … and such. And thanks for volunteering, Luis and Rock. You're a coupla' princes."

"Le gusto es mio, mi Capitan."

"Still making like a recent arrival, Luis?"

As we left the office, Agosto smiled and said, "From this day forth I shall be known as Prince Galahad."

"Hell, I'm a prince, too. Captain said so."

"You're an intern. I guess you could be my page… maybe shield bearer. Can you play a trumpet?"

24

"Straight answer, Tommy. Has she ever asked you for sex?" Tommy Perdue struggled for the words that would best describe an incident between him and his boss's wife, Maggie Perry.

"It wasn't like…it was like she was…"

"Straight out, Tommy. Did she or didn't she? I should warn you Dorothy says she heard Mrs. Preston invite you to her bed."

"Yes sir…but I didn't do it. Like I tried to say, it was like she was tryin' to bribe me."

"Bribe you?"

"Yes sir. Said she'd reward me if I'd kill those creeps what raped Miss April. She'd asked me before…but never said nothing about…you know…going to bed…having sex."

Perry stared at the huge man before answering. "I believe you, Tommy. You're a good man. Now…as sort of a follow up…far as you know, has Mrs. Perry made an offer of sex to any other men? Postman? Yard man? Pool Man?"

"No sir. I'd have known it. Dorothy watches her pretty close. She'd have told me."

"Okay. One other thing, Tommy."

"Yes sir."

"You understand that my wife has a mental problem… started with the rape. You think the guys who raped April deserve to die for what they did to her and to my wife?"

"Yes sir…they should be dead for what they did."

Perry nodded, "If someone paid you a large sum of money, would you kill them…the three who are left?" Perry's eyes narrowed as he waited for a reply.

"I don't know…only ever killed one guy…in a bar fight. Did time for that…course you knew 'bout that when you hired me."

"Just a hypothetical question, Tommy. Let me ask you one other hypothetical question."

"Yes sir."

"If someone you admired…a person who liked and respected you…who needed your help to right a wrong, would you be willing to kill for that person?"

"No money? Just for a friend what needed help?"

"Let's say that some payment would be involved, but mainly it would be to help a friend."

"Put it that way…maybe I would. Probably would."

"You're a good man, Tommy. I always enjoy posing hypothetical questions and evaluating responses. Helps me in my line of work."

* * *

I had a lot of free hours until it was time to hook up with the Lieutenant for the safe house stake out. So, the Saturday after the strategy session in the Captain's office, I again found myself in Donna Infante's neighborhood. Also found myself at her door knocking. Also knew it wasn't accidental…that is, like being in her neighborhood on one of her days off.

She responded quickly. Curly brown hair freshly washed and shining, bright blue eyes dancing, dimples dimpling, she said, "Rock. Come in… please come in." She took my hand and led me to the kitchen where something lovin' was baking in the oven.

I sat down and said, "I'm not interrupting anything am I? In the neighborhood and thought I'd drop by to see how you're doing."

"So nice of you, Rock. I've been hoping you'd stop by again...and you're not interfering with any plans I have. I'm just baking some cakes for our church festival tomorrow."

"Smells delicious. Only time I smell anything that good in the kitchen is when I go home to mom's for a meal... maybe once a month. Ham and cheese sandwiches and Campbell's soup don't do much to stimulate the salivary glands."

"Horrors. You stop by here every Saturday morning and I promise to stimulate the heck out of you." She blushed, put her small hand to her mouth and added, "I mean... stimulate your...taste..."

I found myself roaring over her show of embarrassment. Before I knew it, she was laughing with me. Tears ran down her cheeks. When the laughter subsided, she said, "Could I incite you with a piece...of cake."

We both indulged in another round of laughter before I accepted her offer of a "piece" of cake--chocolate with fudge icing--three layers and five inches high. She cut the cake and put a huge slice on the table in front of me. She poured two cups of coffee and sat down across from me.

As I ate, she seemed to get a huge thrill at the sight of me stuffing my face.

Finished, I wiped my mouth with a napkin she'd provided and smiled at her. "That was great, Donna. You know the way to a man's heart."

"Do I?" A serious expression captured her face. "Something I want you to know, Rock. Please don't laugh at me."

"Of course not."

"Angelo and I…we never…you know…"

"Hold it, kid. I don't need to know what you and Angelo did or didn't do."

"When we laughed at what I said about stimulating you… I was afraid you'd think badly of me. Think I was being crude. I'm not a prude, Rock. But I'm not a free wheeler when it comes to my social life. I just want you to know that Angelo and I were just good friends…nothing beyond that. He needed company and I needed company."

"Like I said, Donna…hey, do you mind if I call you Midge."

"Midge? Funny that you'd ask that. Dad called me Midge. You're not a reincarnation of Dominic Infante, are you?"

"Your father's dead?"

"An accident. He was a iron worker and was killed ten years ago when a scaffolding collapsed."

"Sorry...Midge." I reached out and took her hand and said, "There's something I've got to tell you. I hope you won't be offended."

"What's that, Rock?"

"I'd like to replace Angelo as your special friend."

She smiled and pulled my hand to her cheek, "I'm flattered, Rock. Now I've got something else to tell you. The day that the Lieutenant introduced you, and I looked up into your very serious, very handsome face, I knew I wanted to...no...just had to see you again."

Slowly standing, I walked around the table. She stood and I pulled her close. Her head lay against my chest, and we stood silently immersed in a contentment spawned by an unforeseen union of our minds and bodies. I found myself feeling something I hadn't felt for almost nine years. I knew I couldn't be falling in love as long as April was alive. Or could I? Was Donna...Midge...just a substitute for the sister I always wanted and never had? A sister to love, to protect, to teach me to dance, to indoctrinate me in the ways of the feminine mind? A sister with whom I could exchange secrets?

I buried my face in her hair. It smelled fresh, lightly scented. Then I whispered, "You said something about a church festival tomorrow. Could I wangle an invitation?"

"Can you bake?" she said, "try to wangle your way out of it, friend."

25

It was after seven p.m. and dark. April Perry wondered why any sane person would want daylight savings time. Who would want darkness at night after work instead of in the morning before work? She had worked late--again-- and fully understood why she spent so many late hours in her office. There was nothing for her outside the office. Absolutely nothing. Nada.

She had alienated her father. They still spoke, but that was about it. No chummy daughter and father get togethers for lunch--for anything. Her mother was barely rational. Broke into tears when she went home. All she had to say was "Hello mother", and the tears would flow. The wailing would start. Then there was Rock--only a haunting memory now. How could you love someone and hate what he was? There was no one, nothing else but her work and that was stifling. She had turned into a mean bitch and knew it. What better way to say "hands off" than being a mean bitch?

She entered the municipal parking garage and took an elevator to the third deck. The building was full of shadows and smelled of exhaust fumes, oil droppings, and burned rubber. She walked quickly toward her Jaguar. She reached the vehicle, which was backed into a small car space. Taking out her keys, she pressed the button that unlocked the doors. She reached for the handle and tried to hurry as she heard the soft sound of sneaker-shod feet from behind. From the past. Before she could turn, a strong arm reached around from behind and clutching fingers ripped her keys from her grasp. Wheeling around to face her attacker, her fear mounted as she recognized him. "Josh…you. You bastard. Give me my keys and get the hell away from me."

"Did I scare you, April Baby?" He dangled the keys in her face. Fear and anger gripped her. She began to tremble uncontrollably.

"Give me my keys…you foul bastard."

"Bastard? Oh my, aren't we brave. So insulting…after all that we've shared. Did you enjoy it the last time we got together? The time I had you…twice. I was the first and the last. Did you know that? I really enjoyed you. So young. So inexperienced. And do you remember the time you bloodied my nose and knocked me down in front of my friends. I'll never forget that. It made me feel so inferior… so humiliated. Would you like to try it again…hit me… knock me down." He flexed his biceps and smiled.

He reached toward her and she backed away. He ran his hand over her breasts. "You've grown up, April baby… very nice…" A sound echoed through the cold concrete walls. Josh stopped and listened. The sound of the elevator coming up had broken the silence. The doors opened. A man whistled *Amazing Grace*. Footsteps on the concrete. Security? Of course. Josh smiled, backed away, and returned her keys.

"See you, April Baby. Dream about me. I do about you. We'll meet again." He was gone behind a row of vehicles. Perspiring, shaking, she sank into the Jaguar's soft leather seats, closed and locked the doors, and began to sob. She pounded the steering wheel in anger and said, "He needs to be dead…the evil, cruel bastard. Do I remember the last time? Oh, damn you…damn you to hell. Of course I remember. It was the night I died."

26

A two story, 50's style stucco home, the safe house was on a corner lot at the intersection of two residential streets. I arrived near the location at the time Misha Pulaski was due to return. I was in touch with Misha's escort, the officer in the house--Jim Klein--and Lieutenant Agosto, who was parked around the corner in the driveway of a vacant home.

I had parked my vehicle on the street two blocks away and walked to the site. A neighbor whose property abutted the fenced back yard of the safe house had given me permission to use his garage as my cover. A garage window provided a secure view of the back of the safe house. The neighbor--a thoughtful, graybeard with noticeable arthritis--had left a stool for me to sit on during what would probably be a long and uneventful night.

Nothing had happened by midnight. and I left my stool and walked out for some fresh air. I called the Lieutenant for a check, asked what was up and chuckled at his reply. "Nada de particular, amigo. Were you expecting someone?"

***

Agosto cut his connection with Rock and settled back into his seat. He was back into the sterile monotony of waiting out the night. He didn't relax long. He jerked to full alert when something banged into the car's right rear fender. He glanced into the rear view mirrors as he eased his weapon from its holster. Seeing nothing, he carefully opened the driver's side door and slid from the seat to the pavement in a full crouch. He looked in both directions and saw nothing but the barren street. A bat fluttered overhead, chasing insects attracted by the street lights. He moved slowly to his left, toward the source of the sound.

From the passenger side, a kneeling Azrael watched the direction of Agosto's movement before rising and moving toward the front of the car. A silent shadow, Azrael crept slowly forward in the direction that would bring him to Agosto's back.

Agosto reached the source of the sound that had drawn him out. Saw nothing. After looking in all directions once again, he rose from his crouch and started to turn. Half way around, he was jabbed the neck and several thousand volts of electricity sent him to his knees. His weapon fell from his hand, and The butt of Azrael's gun slammed into the back of his head. He fell face forward, no longer a featured player in the emerging drama. Azrael picked up Agosto's weapon and tossed it to the floor of the unmarked vehicle before locking the doors and throwing the keys into shrubbery bordering the driveway

Azrael was pleased with the performance of the newly acquired tazer. A wonderful device. Prepared to move to the second phase of the evening's agenda, the cunning Angel of Death muttered, "Okay. One down…two to go. One permanently,"

* * *

After my last contact with Agosto, I'd remained outside to stretch out some. I stood in the driveway taking deep breaths of a cool breeze that was pushing away the humidity and haze that embraced the night. The rear door of the safe house opened and a small white pup dashed into the yard. Misha was standing in the doorway watching his poodle pause to do its thing. I heard nothing. Not a damned thing.

But I felt it: an electric shock that put me down but not out. The immobilizing shock was followed by a hard blow to the head that put me on my hands and knees. I must have moved, because I received a second blow that deposited me in the land of nowhere. Bells, whistles, flashing lights, and then nothing.

* * *

After putting down Agosto and Paxton, Azrael entered the rear yard of the safe house through a gate. A floodlight illuminated much of the back yard. However, there was a dark triangle next to the house. From the darkness, Azrael snapped his fingers. The playful and curious pup responded without hesitation, bounding happily into the shadow where he was picked up, held and petted by the dark visitor.

Ten minutes passed before Misha came to the porch and whistled. "Fuzzy, come on in. You had enough time out here. I need some sleep."

"What's up?" A voice from inside asked.

"Damn pup's enjoying his free time."

"I'll get him. Get your butt back in here."

"I'll do it. Probably won't come to you."

"Okay. Get him and get back in here."

Misha entered the yard, heard the pup whimper, and walked toward the dark corner where the squirming animal and death waited. "Little devil come here," he coaxed. He took two more steps forward before Azrael released the pup and rose from the shadow.

A scream froze in Misha's throat. He didn't have a second chance to scream. A slug from a silenced weapon slammed into his chest. As he sank to the ground, a second bullet struck his forehead.

Because of the darkness, Azrael made no attempt to recover the shell casings. No sense. The slugs would identify the murder weapon as the same one that had put Donato down. Slipping through the open gate, Azrael jogged into the cover provided by a patch of scrub brush and small live oaks lying immediately behind the developed area. A blue Malibu waited just on the other side of the dense growth.

Azrael had easily reached the street on the far side of the wooded area when detective Klein stepped out of the house and called Misha. Misha didn't respond, but the pup came running from the darkness, tail wagging, ears flapping, and his master's blood on the tip of his nose.

27

Everything around and on me was white. But I wasn't in the Great Beyond. I knew that for sure because a pack of jackals were yacking it up in my head. I groaned and turned slightly to the left, and pain shot through my head and neck. Five feet away smiling into my anguished face was one Luis Agosto. We were sharing a hospital room.

"What are you doing in my dream, Lieutenant?"

"Probably looking for a way out. I've never in my many years been chased by so many beautiful ladies. Is that all you dream about?"

"What else?" I tried to sit, fought vertigo, and returned my head to the pillow. "What happened, Lieutenant?"

"I'm not quite certain, but I'll bet it wasn't good. Nurse said we were admitted around one a.m. Both unconscious. Both with concussions."

"What time is it now?"

"Little hand's on seven and big one's on twelve. I think it's still morning, but time passes so fast when you're having fun."

"Did that bastard...or bitch...get to Pulaski?" I'm still not certain whether the word bastard can cover both genders. Should it be bastardess?

"I haven't asked. But I believe I know," Agosto said.

"Yeah. No one from the department been in?" I asked.

"Understand Klein came in with us. Far as I know he's gone... probably filling out a resignation form." Agosto paused, then said, "Well, look who's here. The chief magistrate and the hangman."

I lifted my head far enough off the pillow to recognize our visitors: The Captain and Major Beryl Tankersly. The Major spoke first. "How're you two misfits doing?"

Never without a light hearted response in untenable situations, Agosto said, "Now...or before you came in?"

"Watch your tongue, you refugee from a cigar factory... unless you're ready to retire."

"Always ready, Major, but can't afford it. Can't save much on a poor campesino's wages."

The Major smiled and turned to me. "How you feeling, Rock?"

"Not as good as I felt yesterday morning, sir." Then, thinking it was time for some serious talk, I asked, "Did Azrael get Pulaski, sir?"

"Yes...I'm afraid he did. Two shots. One to the chest and one to the head. Poor bastard didn't suffer."

"Won't speak for the Lieutenant, Major, but I'm damned sorry I screwed up. Damned sorry."

"Hold it, Detective. In CID, we share the screw ups. We were all in the plan to protect these last three guys, but we didn't plan well enough. You take your share of the blame. Agosto, too. And I'll take my share as will Captain Jackson, Klein and the others involved. We all underestimated this Azrael...this frigging Angel of Death. But we'll get him or her...we won't have this refugee from God knows where running around whacking citizens and cold cocking two of our best men...putting them in the hospital."

Before the Major laid out his position, I had wanted to say that I didn't hear Azrael coming. Wanted to make excuses like a kid after breaking a window. When he finished, I felt somewhat ashamed. It was obvious he wasn't out to fix the blame, and not out to find a scapegoat or two. He just wanted to solve a problem called Azrael.

The Major looked at me and said, "We've talked to the charge nurse. She says the attending physician wants you to stay here in the lap of luxury for a couple days." Looking at Agosto, he added, "Also said the Lieutenant can leave tomorrow morning." He smiled and added, "Why did you do it, Luis? As acting squad leader, you don't need to do stakeouts."

"I wanted to keep an eye on Rock. He's watermelon green, you know. By the way, why does Rock get the extra day? The Doc a woman?" Agosto submitted a smiling complaint.

"Seems as though Rock got hit twice. Pretty severe trauma," Jackson said.

"Harder head," I suppose, Agosto pretended disgust.

"Either that or yours is softer…a diagnosis I'll withhold for the moment," Jackson smiled and then continued. "We've scheduled a press conference for tomorrow morning at ten. I'll want you there, Luis. Rock you can watch on TV."

"So, I'll be able to dodge my moment of infamy," I said.

"Should we send a reporter to interview you here?" Jackson asked.

"I pass, Captain. Let the Lieutenant handle the honors."

Major Tankersly spoke up. "We should allow these two malingerers to get some rest, Dewayne. I assume you've got a plateful. I sure as hell do." The two officers gave us the usual "get better, don't worry about anything, we'll give your best to the folks in the office" and left the room.

"The Major's an all right guy," I said.

"He's that…but the other shoe's going to drop."

"What do you mean?"

"Things are gong to tighten up. Panteras is going to become the cheese in the mouse trap. If anything happens to Frankie boy, all hell's going to break loose. No more nice guy."

PART FIVE

Frankie Panteras faces Azrael

A suicide selects the time of his/her death; and, of course, murderers select the time for others to die. For the remainder, most would prefer to leave it in the hands of the almighty. Keep me guessing Lord.

CBW '07

28

One day into my incarceration in Room 612, Tampa General hospital, the whoozies had abated somewhat. Overnight, however, I had turned into a Tylenol junky. At times, my headaches made me damned testy, and nurses tended to come and go quickly. I tried not to be nasty, but couldn't seem to avoid being abrupt. Very abrupt. All right, nasty.

I'd groped my way to one of those green vinyl institutional torture devices called bedside chairs and found myself wishing for a cigarette. I'd never smoked, but I needed a fix of some sort. I got one.

"Hello, Rock," she said as she entered the room. She walked to my side, and kissed my cheek. "Heard you were laid up. Thought a visit from me might shock you into a survival mode."

"April…what a surprise. The greatest surprise ever."

"I'd hoped you'd say something like that."

"Seeing you is the best medicine in the world. Sit please," I said and pointed to another of the ugly devices. A brown one.

"May I sit on the bed?"

"Be my guest. The sheets are clean. Lie down if you like."

April smiled and sat down. Her long legs barely touched the floor from the bed's cranked up position. Her knees were within touching distance. Lovely legs. Lovely knees. No touching.

"I heard what happened, Rock. I'm so sorry."

"Aren't you a little pleased?"

"Why should I be pleased?"

"Well…three of the punks who attacked you have paid the ultimate."

She responded honestly. "I do feel a sense of…maybe pleasure's a bad word…perhaps satisfaction's a better one. Does that make me sound like a cold bitch, Rock?"

"Hardly…considering the circumstances. To be totally frank, April, my job is to protect these guys who hurt you…to find out who's killing them. And there's one hellish conflict there. Believe it. They hurt someone I loved…a slender, lovable and lovely child who could turn me into her slave with a dimpled smile. They destroyed a relationship that I've hungered for…dreamed about for over eight years. And the worst thing of all is that…in terms of my feelings for you…I can forget what happened…but you can't. I think it cut your heart out…destroyed your ability to respond to love. A man's love."

She dropped her eyes and folded her hands on her lap. "Do you believe I could be a murderer, Rock? Be honest, please."

"Let me answer this way, April. The motive for the murders has become very apparent. Your rape. You…or someone very close to you… bear the heaviest burden of suspicion. You, your father, mother, a hired gun, Tommy Perdue…maybe…have to be the focus of the investigation. I know that's not news to you. And God knows, I don't want it to be you or anyone in your family. That's a long answer to a short question. Sorry."

"An honest answer. I didn't expect anything else from you, Rock. When did you find out about the rape? I know it never made the local papers, and my family never told you."

"After Davidson was shot, my partner at the time, Rich Martino, recognized him as one of the five."

"Corporal Rich Martino? I remember him. He was the officer who… who found me after the rape. He came to see me several times…in the hospital and at home before I left for Boston. A very sweet man. A caring man."

"Yeah. A good cop. He retired a few weeks ago. Right after the Davidson murder."

April stood up. "I'd better go and let you get some rest."

"Rest? That's the last thing I need or want."

"What do you need and want, Rock?"

"You know damned well what I need and want. You, damn it. You."

"Even if I'm a murderer?" She asked and a sad smile touched her lips.

"Even then, April, Even then." She leaned over and brushed my lips with hers.

"I've always loved you, Rock. But you deserve a whole woman. I'm not that."

"Whole or half, who gives a damn. I don't. Half of April Perry is all I need."

"Bye, Rock. Maybe…we can get together…after… after all this goes away."

For the first time since she walked into the room, my head began to pound. I stood and reached over the bed to push the black button that carried the white imprint of a nurse's cap. My personal Angel of Mercy.

* * *

April left me feeling half angry, half hopeful, and totally confused. I didn't have much time to examine that confusion. I heard the click of high heels on the terrazzo floor.

"You've come back," I said without opening my eyes.

"You must be talking about that beautiful lady I saw leaving your room. Myself, I just got here."

"Oh…my God. Midge." My eyes opened and I was looking into the pixie face of my newly acquired best friend.

"Who was she, Rock?"

"An old friend."

"She didn't look so old to me. Was it April Perry?"

"Yes. What caused you to think it could be April?"

"Angelo told me about you and her in high school. And about how sorry he was…"

"Let's not talk about April. Let's talk about you…how did you find out I was here?"

She kissed me on the forehead and took my hand. "You're not the only detective in this relationship, friend. I've got a bloodhound's nose."

"Hardly. More like a poodle's."

"Funny man."

171

"So how...Miss Bloodhound?"

"We had a date Sunday...remember."

"Damn. The church festival."

"Right. When you didn't show up, I was disappointed at first. Then I decided you weren't the kind of man who'd stand up his special friend on their first date...even though it wasn't what you might call a first date...so I thought something bad must have happened so I..."

"Slow down, Midge."

She giggled and squeezed my hand. "I called the Lieutenant this morning. He told me about it...oh you poor thing...how's your head? Does it hurt? Can I get you an ice pack?"

I took her hand and brought it to my lips. "Just stay with me for awhile, kid. If I go to sleep, it's not boredom. It's contentment. It's so nice to have a special friend...even one with a poodle nose.

29

The hospital was behind me. All gone. The odor of stale coffee, antiseptics, fouled sheets, and urinals waiting to be emptied. When I entered the squad room on the Wednesday morning after the Sunday morning debacle, someone whistled, and another lonesome admirer applauded feebly. I hadn't made the top ten on anyone's hit parade yet. I was just an intern detective who'd blown an assignment.

I knew there had to be some empathy out there. Most of the guys had an element of humanity lurking in their Neanderthal brains. If that sounds unkind, it best reflects a definite lack of enthusiasm over returning to work. My headaches were coming and going. Easing then pounding. The shaved and stitched areas on my scalp were starting to itch. Painkillers still had a firm grip on my get up and go.

A note on my desk proclaimed the Lieutenant's desire to see me. I groaned, tossed the note into an empty wastebasket, and headed for his office. He was waiting.

"I just called Sheila to see if you were in. How you feeling?"

"Okay."

"Liar."

"Okay. Stretched out. Something like the southbound end of a earth worm that's heading north."

"Very graphic. You make it up?"

"Read it somewhere."

"I'd suggest you forget it."

"Done. What's up?"

"Quick review. We had a big meeting yesterday morning. The Mayor was there along with the Commissioner, DA and City Council chairperson. Went pretty well…considering there were politicians present. Mayor was sensational. Said great stuff like 'the murders were giving the city a bad reputation', and 'the Attorney General is looking over my shoulder', and 'the City Council is on the verge of pouncing on someone.' That was clarified by the Chairman of the Council who said they were about to pounce on someone *hard*."

"Pounce? Sounds feline."

"Maybe he said that they were prepared to kick the pee out of someone."

"That sounds diuretic." My responses reflected a deep down desire to bite pointing fingers.

"Anyway, after the politicos left, we discussed the problem posed by the lack of evidence, our failures to date, and ways to protect the remaining targets...Panteras and Sampson."

"Now it sounds interesting. So...?"

"We're faking a move for Panteras and his wife. We have a place on North Dale Mabry...a small ranch style place in the middle of some vacant acreage. We're moving them today or before noon tomorrow."

"Broad day light move? Does that make sense?"

"Relax, amigo. Like I said, it's a put on. Panteras and his wife Mattie will get in an SUV with tinted windows. They'll be accompanied by four of our people...a woman detective...Nan Delacorte, a young detective who resembles Frankie, and Detectives Klein and Nicholson. They'll pull into the garage, and our people will go into the house. When the SUV leaves the garage, only the driver will be visible. Frank and Hattie will be out of sight...on the floor. "

"You named all of the house party except the young guy who looks like Frank. Does he have a name?"

"He does. As I recall, it's a young fella' named Payton… no…Paxton.

Brad Paxton. You know him?"

"Sounds familiar. Should he bring his tooth brush, razor and clean skivvies?"

"Absolutely."

"So what happens to Panteras and his wife?"

"They go to a hotel room that's been arranged and stocked with cops."

"That's it? We put four men in a house and expect to fool Azrael into making a play?"

"That's it. So. What do you think…about the plan, Rock?"

"The truth?"

"Of course."

"I think it…uh…stinks."

"It was Major Tankersly's idea."

"Sorry. Then it's odoriferous. I don't see a plan. I see an activity."

"This might surprise you, but I see it the same way. It's like fishing without bait."

"Like setting a mousetrap without cheese," I said.

"Exactly. Want to hear something else?"

"Yeah. Another plan."

"The Captain doesn't like it either. He asked me to seek a consensus and report back to him."

"He'll take it to Tankersly? Amazing. Gutsy."

"You got it."

"How many opinions do you have?"

"Including you, everyone assigned to implement *the plan.*"

"How many opposed? Let me guess. Everyone assigned to implement the plan." I said. "When will we know if it's on or off?"

"I'll give the Captain my report. He'll call me back after he talks to Tankersly."

"That's it for now?"

"That's it."

"Okay. Now I've got a question…something's that's been bothering me since I regained consciousness," I said.

"Yeah?"

"How in the name of…"

"How did Azrael know when he could get to Pulaski?"

"Yeah. How?

"Observable routine."

"Please explain."

"The puppy. Every night before he hit the sack, Misha put the pup out for a pee and a romp. Midnight on the dot for the ten nights before the hit… according to Klein.

Azrael observed the routine and used it to take poor Misha down."

"But…what about us? It was our first night on stake out."

"Must have anticipated the additional help, and scouted us out before doing the hit. Had five hours to adjust…from seven to midnight. It's the only thing that makes sense… unless there's someone inside."

"You don't believe that."

"Nope. Unless the perp is you," Agosto said, his expression sober.

"Sure. I belted myself on the head twice and shot myself in the back with a tazer."

"Aha…a confession at last." The phone rang and he picked it up. "Right Captain. The consensus…actually everyone…is opposed. Yes. Opposed. I sympathize, Dewanye. By the way, Rock has confessed to the Azrael murders. No lie. No, I didn't torture him. Yes. I agree. If we have to go through with the plan, we'll have something to do…since the perp will be on ice. Good luck, partner."

30

Agosto's perseverance had finally overcome the obstacles--legal and political--that Preston Perry had erected to prevent us from talking to Maggie Perry and the household staff. We had a ten a.m. appointment. It was ten. I lifted the gigantic bronze ring, smiled at the Lieutenant, and let it fall. The sound had barely stopped resonating through the big hall before Dorothy opened the door. Wearing the gray dress, white apron and collar, and an angry face, she waited for Agosto to say something.

"I'm Lieutenant Luis Agosto, Tampa Police Department,

and I believe you know Rock."

"I know Mr. Paxton."

"We have an appointment with Ms. Perry."

"I know. Please come in. She's waiting for you in the activity room. I'll have Tommy take you there." She left us and went into a small room off of the foyer. We heard her talking. Two brief sentences. Probably, "They're here. Come and get them."

Tommy Perdue arrived in a matter of minutes and motioned for us to follow him by lifting his hand and crooking an index finger the size of a Costa Rican banana. We followed him through double glass doors that opened onto the pool deck. Then we followed him around the pool to a set of similar doors, which he opened and held open for us. The activity room was a carpeted room of substantial size. It contained every type of equipment designed by man to exercise and torture the human body. Maggie Perry was pounding a treadmill wearing tight red shorts and a tighter red top. Her attire allowed a full evaluation of her fitness. From ankles, to calves, to thighs, to buttocks, to abdomen, etceteras, Maggie Perry was an outstanding physical specimen. I looked at Agosto. He was staring at Maggie who caught his eye, smiled, and said, "I hope you don't mind if I finish this exercise...I just have five minutes left." Despite a rather fast pace, her breathing seemed regular and unforced.

"No problem, Ms. Perry." He glanced around, spotted a padded bench, and said, "We'll just take over that bench, if you don't mind." We headed for the bench and Tommy followed. He stood behind us, a human monolith. Towering. Silent.

I looked at Agosto and said, "I think we were granted permission to interview Tommy. It might be a good time."

"Right...hate to miss the rest...but we should make the best use of our time." We both turned to face Tommy. "You know that the Counselor said it would be okay to interview you? Said he cleared it with you?"

"Yeah. He tol' me. I said okay."

"We'll be taping the interview. He tell you that, too?"

"Yeah. It's okay. I ain't done nothing."

"That's a good place to start, Perdue. How long have you worked for the Perry family?" Agosto asked.

"Two years before Miss April got herself...raped. Almost eleven years now."

"What are your responsibilities? Have they been defined in any sort of contract...employment agreement?"

"No agreement or contract. Handshake between gentlemen."

"There must be some sort of understanding."

"Like what?"

"Like…well…if your job is to protect the family, wouldn't you need to carry a weapon, Tommy? A sap… knife…gun?"

"My fists are all I need…mostly."

"Have you ever carried a weapon?"

"Knife once…pocket knife."

"Never owned a firearm?"

"Said before, I don't need to carry one."

"I didn't ask if you needed one. My question was pretty simple. Have you ever carried one?"

"Long time ago…I guess. Had a little twenty-two revolver."

"Still have it?"

"Somewhere."

"Let's move on…"

"If you're ready for me, Lieutenant, I'm ready for you." Maggie was behind us, face flushed, a towel draped over her shoulders.

"If you'd prefer to shower first, Ms. Perry, we can finish up with Tommy."

"Oh…good. I feel so damned yucky."

"Fine." Agosto had turned off the recorder. As Maggie retreated, he turned it on and continued Tommy's interrogation.

I followed Maggie to the pool entrance doors and watched as she showered at a poolside shower before diving into the aqua water. I watched in amazement as she did sixteen quick laps of the fifteen meter pool: four lengths using a brisk crawl stroke; four, backstroke; four, breast stroke; and four, butterfly. Completing her regimen, she left the pool and entered a door that, I assumed, was to a dressing room. I returned to where Agosto was still hammering away at Perdue.

"Let me ask again…what are your hours? You know… like eight to five….noon to midnight?"

"Hours are when someone needs me."

"Anytime then?"

"You got it."

"Are you ever asked to drive one of the family?"

"Yeah. Ms. Perry goes shopping, I always drive."

"You ever asked to drive someone at night?'

For the first time, the monolith moved something besides his lips. He fidgeted. "Yeah…once in a while."

"Late at night?"

"Uh…yeah…once in a while."

"Who specifically?"

"I…well…don't remember."

"Don't remember or don't want to say?" Perdue remained silent. Agosto followed up. "Did the Counselor coach you? Tell you to say you didn't remember if you didn't like the question?"

"He said I didn't need to answer some questions...like if they hurt the family."

"Now what did he mean by saying that? What could you say that could hurt the family?" By now, Perdue was shifting his weight from foot to foot and clenching and unclenching his hands.

"Don't know what he meant."

"Oh...you never witnessed anything that might embarrass someone in the family."

"I don't remember."

"When was the last time you took anyone out late at night?"

"I don't remember?"

"Bad memory huh?"

"I guess it's bad sometimes...took a lot of shots to the head. Maybe that's why...uh...here comes Ms. Perry." His relief at the Maggie's arrival was obvious.

"Are you finished with Tommy, Lieutenant?" Maggie asked.

"For now, Ms. Perry. He seems to have had a sudden loss of memory. But we can give him some time to think about...what he knows and exactly what he remembers. May have to have him come down town later this week. In fact, I'll have Detective Paxton check his availability with you before we leave."

"Then...you're ready for me?" She fingered her damp hair and smiled at Agosto. I walked away with Tommy Perdue.

31

I left the activity room--i.e., sweat shop--with Tommy Perdue. Told him that I'd like to interview Dorothy. He took me to a small room off the kitchen. The room had a small table, a bookcase, and assorted lounge furniture. I assumed it was a break room for the staff. Dorothy was sitting at the table drinking coffee. She glanced up and flashed a smile, the first smile I'd ever seen on the face of the rather stoic maid.

"Like some coffee, Rock?"

"Smells great."

"Sounds like a 'yes' to me," she said. She got up, went to the kitchen, and returned carrying a tray holding a pot of coffee, sugar packets, and a creamer.

She placed the tray on the table, and I sat across from her. "You seemed in a rather bad mood at the door this morning, Dorothy."

"You noticed. Yes, I was. Won't deny it. And, call me Dot, please. I'm Dorothy when they want to put on the dog."

"Care to talk about what had you upset?"

She remained silent for a moment before asking, "Between the two of us and the furniture?"

"I can speak for myself...not for the furniture. Yes... between the two of us. One caveat...you know I'm a cop, and you know why I'm here. So, you also know what you can say that can't be privileged."

"Anything that could implicate any of the family in the murders."

"You've got it, Dot."

"It's Maggie...Ms. Perry."

"What about, Maggie?"

"It's her acting."

"Acting?"

"When Mr. Perry's around...or April...the doctor... sometimes she gets weepy. Acts helpless...like she doesn't understand things. Sometimes she's so bouncy, happy and thoughtful she gets on my nerves. Other times she'd moody, sulks…can't be satisfied. Throws stuff and I have to clean up. That's what happened this morning. At breakfast with the Counselor. Said the coffee was too strong and threw the cup across the room. Doctor Wilhelm says she has a psychosis."

"Doctor Wilhelm a psychiatrist?"

"He says he is. I know he's padding his wallet."

"Why do you say that?"

"I'm with her more than anyone. I think she's what my grandma would've called a schemer. Does things for a purpose. Lies. Cries. Has tantrums."

"You don't like her?"

"Used to…she changed after April went North. She used to be sweet…caring. Change came gradually."

"Why do you stay?"

"My husband had an accident…paraplegic now. Can't make forty-five thousand a year doing anything else. Plus we get rent free lodging…cottage on the back of the property."

"Let me see if I understand what you're telling me."

"Okay."

"Maggie puts on an act to convince people she's unstable. The doctor is convinced she has a psychosis. Bipolar, maybe."

"Bipolar…that's what the doctor told the Counselor."

"But you think her mood swings are acting…planned?

"That's what I think. I looked up bipolar. It doesn't sound like her."

"You're saying it's something worse?"

"I'm no psychiatrist, but I don't think bipolar describes her…like I said."

"Do you believe she's capable of killing someone?"

"I don't know. I really don't…hate to believe that about her."

"Does she leave the house at night?"

"I think so…but can't swear to it. I go to the cottage after dinner …eight thirty or so. I've seen cars leaving the grounds late at night, but can't say who's in them."

"Would Tommy know?"

"I'd bet on it."

* * *

Dot called Maggie for me, and Maggie handed the phone to Agosto. "You finished, Lieutenant?" I asked.

"For now," he said. "How about you?"

"I'll be ready to move as soon as we arrange Tommy's appearance downtown."

"You won't have to do that. Maggie's been nice enough to say she'll come down with him on Monday…at Ten."

"How nice," I said. "I'll be waiting for you up front."

32

We left the Perry mansion and headed downtown. I suppose we both had things to think about before we discussed our impressions. Agosto spoke first.

"What's your take?"

"Overall or on my interview with Dorothy?"

"Start with Maggie."

"She's one helluva physical specimen...fully capable of handling the physical side of doing the deeds. "

"I agree."

"She's highly motivated when it comes to conditioning.

I wonder about the motivating factor. Fighting off middle age or something more sinister. Most people at twenty can't do what she's doing at...forty five? "

"I asked her about her age...delicately. She says forty-four. Says she was eighteen when April was born."

"Child bride...holding her age well. Did you ask about her physical fitness program?"

"I did. She said she got a trainer and started a conditioning program a month after April's rape. She says if April had been more physically inclined and less cerebral, she could have defended herself."

"Hell...April was on the volley ball team...seemed fit to me. But volley ball's a team game. She was on her own. Five to one isn't good odds in any sport."

"Maggie doesn't understand sports."

"I'll bet she does. So what else did you get out of your interview with her?" I asked.

"Lot of small things. Seems very outgoing. Straightforward. But I felt it was a veneer. I felt she could manufacture a four page lie without winking a lid."

"Dorothy would agree. She thinks Maggie's an actor... a schemer. She heard the doctor mention bipolar to the Counselor and looked it up. Says it doesn't sound like her. Did Maggie tell you she'd been diagnosed as bipolar?"

"Not specifically. Said she was under a doctor's care for depression. But she was one happy sweetheart during the interview. Turned on all the charm."

"She come on to you?"

"You could say that."

"I could, but can you?"

"Wise guy. Sounds as though Dorothy impressed you."

Agosto said.

"She did. Lady's got problems with Maggie. I think she'd quit in a nanosecond if she could afford to."

"What kind of problems?"

"For starters, her husband's a paraplegic…in a wheel chair. It's an expensive proposition for her. She needs the kind of income and benefits she gets here and couldn't expect to get anywhere else. Counselor treats her fine. Like I said, her problem's with Maggie."

"How old is she?"

"Didn't ask and I'm no good guessing ages. Once I thought thirty was over the hill. You saw her…what do you think?"

"I'd say fifty-five…around there," Agosto said."

"About your age, oh ancient one?"

"How'd you like to walk? Oh wise-assed one?"

* * *

When we got to the station, we learned that the Major had called a meeting of all the principals in the Azrael murders: Captain Jackson; ME Dr. Milton Bosch; Dr. Winifred Larson, head forensics tech and her boss, Dr. Agnostic Broadhurst; Detectives Jim Klein, Mike Nicholson, Nan Delacorte, Shane O'Malley, and, of course, Agosto and me.

The Lieutenant and I entered the specified conference room. Major Tankersly was sitting at the head of a large conference table. Captain Jackson sat to his left, and Milton Bosch, to his right. Agosto slipped into the chair beside his old buddy Bosch. I sat next to Agosto. The other four detectives straggled in and paired off.

All were present when the Major glanced at his watch and said, "Okay. Everyone's here…and on time. Good. I've ordered coffee and some rolls. Should be here shortly. Might as well get started. Captain Jackson, kick it off."

Jackson nodded and began. "You're all aware of the decision to abort the original plan after I reported your views to Major Tankersly. He was very pleased that we spoke up. Said he, too, had second thoughts about it. He has asked that we review the situation and come up with an alternative plan. I'm going to start around the table and ask each of you to state any specifics that seem relevant based on your part in the investigation. Milton you lead off."

Bosch cleared his throat and began. "I believe all here know what we learned from the autopsies. All three victims died from gunshot wounds. Only one victim was shot more than once. Pulaski. And I don't believe a second shot was necessary in his case. The killer's accuracy is noteworthy, considering that in two instances the lighting was poor and the kill shots struck the chest left of center and entered the heart. That's it. The killer can use a weapon."

"Dr. Larson, please."

"Yes sir. All of the recovered projectiles and shell casings indicate two weapons were used. Davidson was shot with a 9mm, S&W Model P230. A 9mm Sig Sauer Model P228 was used in the last two murders. In addition, we have the hair strand, which was found on a chair at the Angelo Donato murder site. It was three inches long, of natural black coloration and from a female. No root, so we're limited to a mitochondria DNA comparison. We've obtained hair samples from all of Miss Infante's female friends, but have yet to receive a sample from two suspects…Maggie and April Perry. No matches to date. The blue cotton blend thread recovered from the shrub at the Donato sight has been identified as a type used in the manufacture of sweat suits. Athletic shirts. Very common. Many outlets."

"Anything else, Doctor?"

"No, Captain."

"As senior detective on the case, Luis. Please run through the procedures followed before and after the murders."

"I'm certain all are aware of the circumstances prevailing in the Davidson case. The only evidence recovered at the site was a shell casing...one of three. We interviewed individuals living in neighboring apartments. Several heard the burglar alarm, one couple heard a car take off...burning rubber...about the time the alarm started. We found evidence of that, but nothing to distinguish a type of tire. On the Donato case, Angelo received a death threat from Azrael. We took what we thought were adequate precautions. Donato was told to stay in his house until we could arrange full time protection. At seven thirty a. m., he arrived at his girl friend's house about the same time we discovered that he'd left his home, but didn't have a clue as to where he'd gone..."

"Lieutenant?"

"Yes, Detective Delacorte?"

"We've heard that his employer knew where he'd be. Why wasn't he contacted?"

"We placed several calls to Mr. Corelli. Didn't make a connection until...I think it was around ten."

"Seems as though Azrael knew more about Donato's habit patterns than...uh...we did."

"He certainly did…and if you're suggesting *we* screwed up, maybe *we* did. But face it, Nan, Rock and I weren't gifted with your apparent superb hindsight."

"I wasn't saying that. You seem damned sensitive…"

"Okay, you two. Can it. I'll get the coffee and rolls in here and we'll take a fifteen minute break." Major Tankersly doused the conflagration.

33

During the break, Nan Delacorte apologized to Agosto. In return, he admitted a elevated level of sensitivity over our failure to protect Donato. After the break, Agosto completed his observations. "In the Pulaski killing, Azrael demonstrated flexibility. Found we'd anticipated a switch in targets and doubled our coverage at the safe house. He or she did a preliminary check, spotted Rock and me, and put us down before doing Pulaski. Also used a tazer for the first time. We need to investigate possible sources and purchases of the item. Need to check it out with our street people. That's it from my end, Major."

After thanking Agosto, the Major said, "Okay, we've covered the history of our failures and agreed that this bastard or bastardess is clever, tenacious, and committed to the task of wiping out the five punks who raped April Perry. As far as we know, we have two targets left…Josh Sampson and Frank Panteras. We haven't heard from our killer since the Pulaski hit, but even if we do get a message, we're not going to be suckered again. We've got to plan as though we have no idea who's the next victim. Any ideas?"

Awareness of the adage "Fools rush in where Angels fear to tread" didn't deter me from opening my mouth. "I believe we need to change our emphasis."

"In what way, Rock?"

"We've unsuccessfully focused on protecting the rapists. Perhaps, we should concentrate on our suspects. We have three…maybe four. Go to 24/7 surveillance of the four."

"Take a lot of manpower," the Major said. "Any thoughts about Rock's proposal?"

"Don't think there are any guarantees either way," Klein said.

"I believe Rock's right," Agosto said.

"I agree," Nan Delacorte said and smiled at the Lieutenant.

The Major polled the rest and found a surprising consensus. "Okay, we'll reduce our focus on protecting the two remaining rapists and go to a full-time surveillance of our three prime suspects: Maggie, Preston, and April Perry"

"Major."

"Yes, Rock?"

"I believe Tommy Perdue should be added to the list of suspects. I don't believe he's Azrael, but he may be assisting in some way."

"Any disagreement? None. I'm going to ask Captain Jackson and Lieutenant Agosto to develop and distribute a twenty-four/seven schedule for the two functions... surveillance and protection, borrowing men from other units as necessary...Captain Jackson will arrange that. Slightly altered protection procedures should be made daily. Also, Agosto and Paxton will take the additional assignment of coordinating and monitoring all aspects of the new plan. You have any additional thoughts, Captain Jackson?"

"I do, Major. For security, no paper work...schedules and assignments should be posted. All will be hand delivered to the affected personnel. Any comments? Questions? You're dismissed except for the Lieutenant and his partner. "

I could see a lot of hours on the job and very few hours with my very special friend. I found myself thinking of

Midge more than was right for a guy still in love with April.

34

Azrael noted the change in emphasis by TPD several days after it began and decided it was time to write two notes. First to Frankie. Then, of course, to Sampson:

HI FRANKIE!
WERE YOU DISAPPOINTED BY MY SWITCH TO MISHA? I THOUGHT YOU MIGHT BE. BUT DON'T WORRY. I'LL GET AROUND TO YOU. MAYBE JOSH FIRST. THEN YOU. OH. HOW'S MATTIE DOING? WOULDN'T WANT ANYTHING TO HAPPEN TO MATTIE. AND I THINK YOUR PARENTS LIVE IN TOWN. FRANKIE, SR. AND MARIA. SWEET PEOPLE.

BUT SWEET PEOPLE DIE EVERY DAY. SEE YOU SOON. SUGGEST YOU ALL SHOULD TALK TO A PRIEST.

AZRAEL - ANGEL OF DEATH

Azrael folded the note to Panteras, placed it in an envelope, and sealed it--taking the precaution of wetting the seal with a moistened sponge. "Now one for Josh. This will be great fun," the Angel smiled and wrote the second note:

HI MUSCLES.

ARE YOU MISSING YOUR GOOD FRIENDS? AND ARE YOU RIGHT WITH YOUR MAKER? THINK YOU SHOULD PLAN ON AN EARLY DEMISE. HEAR YOU HAVE A GIRL FRIEND. ANTONIA. KEEP HER AROUND. I MIGHT WANT TO TAKE HER AWAY FROM YOU AFTER YOU PASS ON TO YOUR REWARD. BE SEEING YOU SOON.

AZRAEL ANGEL OF DEATH

* * *

Both letters were mailed from the downtown post office. Both were delivered the following day and opened by the officers assigned to the two men. Both officers used latex gloves. After being read, they were bagged with the envelopes. I was called to pick up the bagged material and deliver it to forensics. This "coordination" duty had turned into gopher work for me and a ton of desk time for Agosto.

Upon returning downtown with the new Azrael notes, I took them to Dr. Broadhurst and requested copies for the Captain and the Lieutenant. He obliged, and I headed for Agosto's office, copies in hand.

Reaching the office, I knocked and received an abrupt response.

"Yeah. Come in if you have to."

"It's Rock, Lieutenant," I said as I opened the door. "I've got something you should see."

"Okay. Come in and sit."

"You sound a trifle ruffled," I said as I laid the copied notes on his desk and sat down.

"Ruffled ain't the word for it. Damned paper work's a pain in the butt. What you got, Rock?"

"Azrael's back in touch."

Agosto read the notes and looked up. "What's your reaction?"

"Number one, I don't think we have to worry about Frankie's family."

"Why not."

"I don't believe Azrael wants to kill anyone but the rapists. Had an opportunity to kill Donna Infante, you, and me. Chose to knock us out instead…even though killing us would have simplified things for him…or her."

"So you think the threats to Frankie's wife and family are only intended to spread our resources thinner than they are?"

"That's what I believe."

"I agree."

"There's something else."

"Yeah?"

"How in the hell did Azrael find out Sampson has a girl friend named Antonia?"

"Good question."

"Lieutenant?"

"Yeah, Rock."

"Do you suppose Sheila could take over delivering schedules… picking up reports?"

"You're unhappy, partner?"

"I'm tempted to dive into open manholes, and there's gopher fur growing on my back."

"So…?"

"I've got a hunch I'd like to follow if I could be freed up for a couple of weeks."

"Have anything to do with Josh Sampson?"

"A lot to do with Sampson…and his girl friend."

"Thought it might. It'll be between you and me…and you'll report in every day by cell phone or in the flesh…or fur."

"Then it's okay?"

"Yeah. On you way out, send Sheila in."

"Thanks Lieutenant."

"Le gusto es mio, compadre."

"I love it when you talk dirty, Lieutenant."

"Yeah. Get the hell out of here before I change my mind."

"Si, amigo, le gusto ain't yours alone," I said.

35

After leaving the Lieutenant's office, I went to my desk and dug out Sampson's home and work addresses and telephone numbers. I wrote them in a small spiral pad. Then I read the interview report, which was--as expected-- full of a lot of arrogant, wise guy crap. I began jotting down the things that made me want to take a closer look at him:

1. Putting on a muscle suit doesn't turn cowards into heroes. And everything I know about him says he's still a coward. He should be afraid, but he's not. Why not?

2. He's a conceited bully and fully capable of holding a grudge against the guys who turned on him, testified against him. Murders didn't start until after he was released. (Note: check on validity of the grounds for early release).

3. What caused him to choose April as his target? Did something happen between them we're unaware of? Check with April--if she'll talk to me.

4. Doubt other suspects could know Josh's girl friend's name. How could they unless they're free to follow him around on a daily basis? Only Maggie Perry has that kind of free time. Any of the suspects could have an accomplice. If Azrael is Maggie or Preston Perry, Tommy Perdue could be the accomplice. If April, who? Maggie? Tommy?

4. An ex-con would be more likely to know--or be able to find--sources of tazers and silencers. Criminal defense attorneys might have contacts for such hardware, but it would be less likely. I should check with the team looking for local sources of regulated items.

Things To Do

1. Make appointment with April.

2. Interview prison guard involved in Josh's early release. Clear with Lt.

3. Get time for Agosto's meeting with Perdue from Sheila. Be there.

4. *Visit marina where Josh works. Talk to Klein. Clear with Lt.*

5. *Interview girl friend. Antonia.*

6. *Check on progress. Source of SG and SIL.*

I Closed my note pad and dropped it into an inside jacket pocket and called April's office. Surprisingly, I reached her without delays.

"This is Attorney Perry."

"April, it's Rock. Do you have a few minutes? Business only."

After a moment's silence, she said, "I'm due in court in twenty minutes. That be enough time?"

"Sure will."

"You outside?"

"No. In the squad room."

"I'll be waiting. Don't waste time getting over here." She hung up, and I practically ran to the parking area.

Eight minutes had passed before I reached the DA's offices. The pool secretary pointed and waved me through. One knock and I was admitted.

"Hello, Rock. You look out of breath. Sit before you pass out."

"Not quite in that bad of condition, April. But I will sit."

"Okay, Detective. How can I help you?"

"This may sound insulting in a way, but it isn't meant to be. I'm interested in finding a reason for Sampson picking you as a victim. My first thought was that it was a payback. I beat the hell out of him once, and he knew you were my...girl...so."

"That may have been part of it, but I think it was something I did."

"Which was?" I asked and she described the confrontation at her locker when she knocked Josh down with her book bag in front of his goons.

"That would do it. With his ego, he had to get even. Had to. Amazing, you actually bloodied his nose and put him on his knees. Wish I could have seen it...and wish I'd been there for you after..."

"But you weren't, were you? Not then. Not later."

"No one would tell me what happened. Where you were."

"I know, Rock. I know." There was a sadness in her voice and on her gorgeous face that I hadn't seen in our earlier meetings. "It was a hundred years and a lot of pain and regrets ago." She laid a soft smile on me and rose from her chair. She was still beautiful: Tall and slender with flawless complexion, dark eyes, and glistening black hair.

She came around the desk as I stood up. She touched my lips with her finger tips and said, "It's good to see you on your feet, Rock. How's the head?"

"Fine. As hard as ever."

"Will you walk with me to the courtroom?"

"Try to stop me. Just try." I walked beside her to the courtroom entrance, as proud as ever to be in her company. One frightening reality degraded the occasion. She could be Azrael. She could be a murderer.

36

After leaving April at the courtroom door, I returned to the squad room to update my notes. On my desk was a reminder to join Agosto in his office for the Tommy Perdue interview at ten-thirty a. m. I looked at my watch. It was ten-thirty-five.

When I entered the office, I was surprised to find Maggie there in full war paint and wearing a brown silk pant suit with gold stitching on the collar.

"Hello, Rock. I almost missed you…and that would have been bad for my morale." Her voice was throaty--

almost sensual--and I think I blushed.

"You're leaving?"

"Yes. Preston and I are shopping for a new vehicle. We thought we could work our way through a few dealerships while Tommy's here."

"Looking for anything in particular?"

"The usual. Jaguars, Mercedes...Preston likes Volvos and I think they're horrible...but we'll compromise and get what I want." She laughed and moved toward the door.

"It's a woman's world," Agosto said. "We should be finished before lunch, Ms. Perry."

The door closed behind her, and I looked at a surly Tommy Perdue who sat at the desk waiting to complete his interview. "Hi, big man. How you doing?" I asked.

"Like you care," was his sullen response.

"Certainly we care, Mr. Perdue. And if you drop the attitude and cooperate, we'll get this over and you can join the Perrys car shopping."

"Okay. Go ahead." His bull neck was a nice shade of pink. I'm certain the Lieutenant was happy that there was a desk between them and that he had me as backup.

"Okay. I'm turning on the recorder. You okay with that?"

"I said it was okay last time."

"You've got a right to change your mind."

"If I did, what?"

"Detective Paxton would take notes."

"So he could put down stuff I didn't say. I trust the recorder more."

"Fine. We were discussing your driving assignments… particularly your night assignments. I hope your memory has improved. Otherwise, it could be a long day for all of us."

"I said you should go ahead."

"When was the last time you took anyone out at night?"

" 'bout a week ago. Took Ms. Perry shopping."

"Where?"

"Mall…Eastwood…I think the name was. Yeah… Eastwood."

"You go in the mall with her?"

"No. Went across the street to a bar. Had a couple of beers."

"She tell you when to return for her?"

"No. Said she'd give me a call. I got a cell phone."

"What time did she call you to pick her up?"

"I don't remember."

"Oops. Wrong answer. Approximately what time?"

"Maybe twelve thirty."

"Mall stays open that late?"

"Don't know how late. I picked her up at that restaurant across from the furniture store."

"At twelve thirty?"

"Coulda' been twelve forty five."

"Any explanation why she took so long?"

"Said she wanted a snack…ran into a friend, and they got to talking like broa…like women do."

"Can you pin down the night you took her to the mall?"

"Last time?"

"Of course. That's the night we're talking about, isn't it?" Agosto pretended impatience.

"It was last Saturday…I guess."

"You guess?"

"It was Saturday. Saturday's the night the Counselor plays cards at his club when he's in town. Sometimes he stays over."

"So…does Ms. Perry usually go out on Saturday? Uh…let me put it this way. Does she go out on Saturday night often?"

"Yeah."

"Do you always drive her?"

"Most of the time…not always."

"Does she spend much time away from the house by herself on weekdays?"

"Not much. Couple days a week...not counting Saturday." Perdue was beginning to fidget.

Agosto hit the stop button on the recorder. "You need to use the toilet, Tommy? Maybe you'd like to take a break... get a cup of coffee."

"Like to use the toilet."

Agosto called Sheila. "Sheila, would you come and pick up Mr. Perdue. He needs to use the WC."

Sheila arrived and Perdue followed her from Agosto's office. After the door closed, he looked at me and smiled, "Seems as though Maggie has moved up on the suspect list."

"Sure does. Saturday just happens to be the night we both got hammered."

"I don't think I'm getting the whole truth from him... but I'm getting enough."

"I agree, Lieutenant. I'd like to see you rattle his cage a little more. About his personal involvement."

"I intend to. I believe he knows a hell of a lot more about the family's comings and goings than he's owned up to."

"Wonder if he knows a source for uncommon hardware?"

"I wouldn't be surprised..." The door opened, and Perdue returned carrying coffee in a Styrofoam cup. The cup looked like a kid's toy teacup in his huge mitt.

"I see Sheila took good care of you, Tommy. She's a great kid."

"Yeah, nice." Perdue reoccupied the chair at Agosto's desk.

"You got a girl friend, Tommy?"

"Yeah. Got a couple."

"See them often?"

"Yeah…once or twice a week. One more than the other."

"You do this when you take one of the family members out? Or you just take a night off?"

"Most of the time when I know she's…Ms. Perry…is going out. She says it's okay to go see them." His girls are probably working girls who reside at the intersection of Florida and Hillsborough avenues was my unspoken comment.

"Oh. Forgot to tell you…the recorder's back on, Tommy. Okay?"

"Okay."

"We talked some about weapons the last time. Remember?"

"Yeah."

"You said you had a twenty-two caliber revolver someplace. Do you remember where it is?"

"Yeah. Found it in a shoe box and gave to the Counselor. Said he'd turn it over to you guys."

"You guys? You mean the police department?"

"Yeah. You guys."

"We can check on that. You know much about weapons, Tommy?"

"Not much."

"You know what a tazer is?"

"Yeah." The pink returned to Tommy's neck. Agosto had touched a nerve.

"Have any idea where someone might buy one?"

"Why ask me? Cops use them…know where to get them."

"Yes, we know where. I asked if you knew. Maybe you know someone on the street who has access to them. Maybe a dealer…maybe a dirty cop from…well…just about anywhere."

"I heard of sources…long time ago."

"Like…?"

"A gun shop in Gibsonton."

"Gun shop still there?"

"Hell…how should I know? I never go to Gibsonton."

"Do you remember if the owner of that gun shop makes and or sells silencers? Sorry. Should have asked. Do you know what a silencer is?"

"Yeah. I know what they are…don't know if he makes or sells them. I never been there. Never asked about tazers and silencers."

"Like you heard but didn't give a damn?"

"Yeah. Like that."

"Let's change direction here, Tommy. I want you to listen very carefully and consider the consequences before responding."

"Consequences?"

"Yes. If you lie about what I'm going to ask you, you could be charged as a party to felony murder…when we catch the perpetrator."

"What's the question?"

"Has anyone in the Perry family ever talked to you about committing a crime or assisting him or her in the commission of a crime?"

"Repeat the question," Perdue said. And Agosto did, carefully and precisely. After he finished, Perdue said, "I need to talk to the Counselor."

37

After Agosto cleared it with Major Tankersly, I traveled north on State Route 301 and arrived at the entrance to Lawtey Correctional after a little over an hour's drive. I was cleared through the gate into the outer compound and told where to park. The normal processes for my clearance into the administrative wing were completed, and I was directed to the Warden's office. There, I was politely received by a female clerical worker, who introduced herself as Nancy something or other. She buzzed the Warden, and a gruff voice from the inner sanctum asked, "Is it the detective from Tampa?"

"Yes sir."

"Send him in." She pointed to the Warden's office door and nodded.

Warden Jack Sesniak was sitting behind his desk. An imposing man--tall and trim--he stood and stuck out a hand. "Welcome to Lawtey, Detective Paxton, best damned facility in the whole damned system."

I accepted the extended hand, accepted the PR comment with some skepticism, and said, "Thanks for seeing me Warden. I should correct one thing."

"Sit and correct, Lad."

"I'm not a detective yet. I'm classified as a Detective Intern."

"Too long. I'll call you Detective…if you don't mind." he smiled and continued. "I heard about the program from Major Tankersly. We go way back. He thinks highly of you…I think he called you Rock. Followed your football career."

"He's kind. It wasn't a very long or spectacular career."

"Long enough to impress Beryl. Okay, you've asked to interview one of our corrections officers, Terry "Deke" Dietrich?"

"Yes sir."

He touched the intercom button. "Nancy. Has Officer Dietrich made himself available yet?"

"Yes sir. He's waiting."

"Good. Send him to the conference room." The Warden leaned back and pointed to a door several feet to the right of the one through which I'd entered his office. "That's the conference room door. It's all yours, Detective."

I thanked the Warden and entered the conference room. Nothing fancy. It's furnishings included a large table, a dozen or so institutional chairs with dark cherry finish and padded brown vinyl seats and backs. There was a coffee bar with two pots half full of very black and very old coffee. Dietrich was sitting and waiting.

Walking toward him, I said, "Officer Dietrich, I'm Brad Paxton. Thanks for seeing me."

He stood and took my hand, shook it briefly, and returned to his chair. I joined him at the table. "You like some coffee Paxton? It's corrosive." He smiled, as I rejected the offer of "corrosive" coffee.

Dietrich was at least six feet tall and solidly built. He had sharp blue eyes under bushy brownish red eyebrows, and red hair with graying sideburns. I thought of my father's weathered face and made an assumption: Dietrich was an outdoorsman.

"You fish?" I asked.

"How'd you guess?" he grinned and ran his hand over his leathery bronze features. "Yeah...I fish anytime I can get away. Call me 'Deke,' Detective. I might not answer to anything else."

"I'm Rock and ditto." I reached across the table and we shook hands again. "I don't know if you were told why I wanted to see you, Deke."

"Something about the incident in the closet with a couple of inmates a couple of years ago."

"That's it. First of all, what started the brawl?"

"I have no idea what started it. It just happened...out of the blue as they say. I was supervising a work detail...four guys mopping floors in the administrative wing, and...like I said...it just happened."

"No words?"

"No words. Nothing."

"Was Josh Sampson one of the four?"

"He was at one end of the hall with another inmate... Pederson...and I was watching two other guys at the opposite end."

"And?"

"One of the men opened a maintenance supply closet door. I assumed he was planning to mop the closet."

"He had other ideas?"

"Bet your sweet patootie he did. The guy behind me... Emmitt Price ...shoved me into the closet. And before I realized what was happening, both of them had me backed into the corner and were hammering the hell out of me. I couldn't get to my baton…the way they were working me over."

"Second guy's name was…?"

"Rafael Camarata. Anyway, they each got in a half dozen shots before Sampson opens the door and grabbed Camarata. Gave him a shot to the gut. Then he pushed me aside and slammed Price into the wall and hit him a time or two."

"That broke it up?"

"Yeah…they both backed away with their hands in the air."

"That seem odd to you?"

"What do you mean?"

"Two cons back away from a fight after two or three punches. Were these guys the type that take a lot of abuse from the other cons?"

"You kidding? Just the opposite. Both of them pumped iron. Like Sampson. They were all tough as wang leather… handled me like I was a ballet dancer. You know…a feminine type."

"Were these two friendly with Sampson…as far as you know?"

"Yeah. Camarata and Sampson were tight. Don't know about Price and Sampson."

"I'll repeat my question. Doesn't it seem odd to you that two guys…who you describe as tough as wang leather… would back off after a couple of shots to the gut?"

"I guess they did give up…sort of easy like."

"Could it have been a set up?"

"Set up?" He paused for a moment, his forehead creased. "I get you. Like they worked it out with Sampson…made it look as though he saved my rear. Yeah…come to think on it…it could have been a set up."

"A set up that earned an early release for Sampson. Right?"

"It did…and damn. I testified and helped him get that early release. It happened…almost two years ago. As I think back, I was so damned grateful to him for saving me from a real whipping…that I didn't see it. Looks as though they made a fool of me and the Parole Board. The punks conned us."

"A probable scenario. What happened to Price and Camarata?"

"Camarata got an additional six months. He's out now."

"And Price?"

"He got added time, but it didn't matter much to him. He still had a minimum of ten to do."

"You don't happen to know where Camarata went after his release, do you?"

"Tampa, I believe. He passed me on the way out. Said if I ever got to Tampa, I should look him up. Then he threw me a kiss and gave me the middle finger."

"No wonder you go fishing as much as you can. It's so clean out there."

"You got it, Rock. Nothing but blue water, blue skies, and fish that fight fair."

We talked about unrelated stuff for a few minutes before I stood up and said goodbye. "Thanks again, Deke. Watch your rear and stay away from broom closets unless you're with friends."

"You got it, Rock. If you ever want to go fishing, give me a call. I'll show you how it's done." He handed me a card that indicated that he was the captain of a party boat.

"Free trip, Deke?"

"Can't make money on freebies, Rock. But call and we'll discuss a reduced rate." We both grinned and parted friends.

38

After leaving Lawtey, I went straight back to headquarters. I put my recorded interview with Officer Dietrich in an envelope. I wrote a short note, and dropped both items on the Lieutenant's desk. It was Friday afternoon, and I had convinced myself I had earned the remainder of the day off. I called Midge and asked her what she was doing. When she said "nothing", I took it as an invitation and headed for Temple Terrace.

She saw me coming and opened the door. She stood there, hands on her hips, and said, "I said I wasn't doing anything. That doesn't mean you can just barge in on me without asking, Rock Paxton. I could be taking a shower… getting ready for a date."

I know my face turned red. Then I thought I saw a giggle in her eyes. I stepped into the foyer, picked her up, kicked the door closed, and carried her to the living room. After depositing her on the couch, I kneeled beside her and kissed her hard.

"You ornery imp. You really had me going. I should leave just to get even."

"Goodbye, Rock." She said as she sat up and straightened her skirt.

"Damn. You are angry."

"No woman likes to be taken for granted, Rock. And I am a woman…in case you haven't noticed." She stood, arched her back, and walked into the kitchen. Her walk was delightfully provocative. I followed her. She kept her back to me, so I wrapped my arms around her and pulled her tight to my chest despite some resistance.

"I'm a stupid ass, Midge. You're right. I have taken you for granted …probably because I'm so comfortable with you. You are a woman…a very desirable woman…and I'm sorry I've been so damned insensitive."

I fell her tremble. I put my hands on her shoulders and turned her around. She turned her face to hide the tears in her eyes. "Look at me, sweetheart," I said.

She turned her head, and as I looked into her tear-dimmed eyes, I knew that my prior apology had lacked the force of feeling. It had been words. Just words. Pro forma. Shame washed over me like a blast of hot desert wind. "Midge…Midge…I am so sorry and so ashamed. You mean a helluva lot to me," I said. Then I hesitated and said something I thought I would never say again, "You are the best thing that has ever happened to me. I believe…no…I know that I love you. God as my witness, I'll never hurt you again."

She blinked the tears from her bright blue eyes--which lacked their typical sparkle--and said, "But what about… her?"

"April?"

"Yes, April."

"April and I are a lovely, faded dream. A dream I've carried with me as an abiding reality for nine years. I've carried it as a shield…a shield to deflect all other romantic attachments."

"Deflecting my shameless advances?" She smiled a little.

"Hardly shameless, Doll."

"What's changed?"

"Maybe I've finally realized that the sharp realities of my teens…as do most such realities…became fantasies somewhere during the passage of time. They were actually just fond memories. Nothing more. Nothing less. I allowed a memory to become a fixation, a fixation that destroyed my ability to function in a normal way. I still have fond memories of April the way she was. But she could never again be the person she was just as I could never again be the person I was."

In completing that confession, I wondered if I'd emoted a soliloquy on April's demise--done it more for my own benefit than for Midge's. A dirge for a lost love? But it was over. I knew it then and, for some reason, I felt relieved.

Midge rose on her tiptoes, her lips open, searching for mine. I obliged. Our kiss became the first of many kisses. Still kissing, I picked her up and carried her from the kitchen to the living room couch where we lay together until the burst of passion subsided. I held her on my lap, stroking her hair, touching her lips.

It grew dark. "Would you like to go somewhere for dinner?" I asked.

"Would you?"

"Not really," I said.

"Neither would I," she said as she repositioned herself in my arms.

* * *

Frankie Panteras insisted that they stop despite Nan Delacorte's attempts to dissuade him. She pulled the unmarked vehicle to the curb in front of the small shop where Frankie purchased his daily pack of cigarettes. Frankie's persistent argument had been persuasive once again: "If you got detectives on all the suspects, how could this punk Azrael do anything without getting caught?"

So once again as she had all week, she watched and waited while Frankie entered the shop. He was the only customer. He sauntered up to the counter and spoke to the clerk who knelt behind it. "Hey, Ahmed. How about a pack of...oh my God. Oh no. Please don't."

A scowling man--who was obviously not Ahmed--rose from behind the counter and fired two quick shots into Frankie's chest. With bloody froth bubbling at the corners of his mouth, Frankie slipped to the floor as his killer left through the alley door at the rear of the shop. Before Detective Delacorte realized that Frankie had been hit, the killer was a block away climbing into a blue Chevrolet Malibu.

* * *

Only three minutes passed before a concerned Delacorte entered the shop, found Frankie, and called for an ambulance and backup. While waiting, she kneeled next to Frankie and asked, with her lips to his ear, "Who Frankie? Did you see who shot you?"

He gurgled, "Didn't...know....Never saw be..." Then his eyes opened wide, and he joined the three fellow rapists who had gone before.

After assuring herself that Frankie was dead, and that she could do nothing to help him, Detective Delacorte went through the small shop, including the storage room in the back where she found the unconscious store owner. After removing some restraints, she splashed cool water in his face and stayed with him until she heard a call from the front of the shop.

"Delacorte. You here?"

It was Agosto's voice. She responded reluctantly, already resigned to the butt kicking that was in the offing. "Back here, Lieutenant," she said. "I'm with the proprietor. He needs help."

* * *

I need to pause and clarify my story as I reach this point nine years after the beginning. A day after I found myself expressing my love for Midge, I discovered something that I thought was a given after two consenting adults expressed a full and loving commitment to each other. Based on my reading and observation of societal norms, I believed that a sexual relationship would be an immediate and prolonged outcome of such a commitment. Wrong. Midge wasn't in sync with the trends. In some ways, I was pleased to discover it. In others? Let's say the frustration had been at times somewhat painful.

I had planned to visit Josh Sampson's PO, but had put that aside until Monday. However, that wasn't what dominated my thoughts. I was, instead, reliving that first exciting encounter with Midge and examining certain options that it presented: Was I willing to consummate my desire--lust if you will--by marrying this desirable imp? Was I ready for marriage? Could I get around her teen vow of purity until marriage? You know. Play it by ear? Wait her out? Probably not.

Well, that's where I was on that day almost nine years to the day from the beginning: Caught up in a series of murders involving those who raped my first great love. And caught up in a new love with an ornery pixie who could play kissy face with a passion, and withhold the normal consequence with bulldog determination.

Despite the pleasure of just lying with Midge in my arms, I had reached a point where the welfare of our budding relationship required my departure. So much is often too much.

When I arrived home at midnight, I headed for the kitchen for a cold glass of anything liquid. Before turning on the kitchen lights, I noticed the red blinking light on the wall phone. Feeling that I needed some privacy with Midge, I'd turned off my cell phone. Therefore, the red light on my home phone spelled trouble. I picked up the phone and the sound of Agosto's voice confirmed the blinking red light's message.

"Where the hell you been, Rock. I've been trying to reach you since late this afternoon. Don't call…just get your butt in here. We've got problems."

39

Detective Nan Delacorte was a tall woman. Wearing flats, she was looking directly into Captain Jackson's eyes when he said, "How could this happen, Detective? You have one man to protect, and he gets popped under your nose. You don't use your weapon . You don't see…"

I had entered the conference room just as the Captain had started in on Nan. When he saw me, he broke off his harangue. I was happy for Nan's sake. "What's up, Captain?" I said.

"Well, Paxton, the Lieutenant finally track you down?"

"Yes sir. He left a message on my home phone. Uh… where is the Lieutenant, sir?"

"The Lieutenant, Klein and Nicholson have been working the crime scene area since six. They went for a bite to eat. I was out of town and just got back. Detective Delacorte wasn't hungry, it seems."

I looked at the crestfallen detective. She was pale, her hair in disarray, and her normally bright, probing eyes were dull. Dead dog tired. "I heard your questions, Captain. I assume Azrael got to Panteras."

"He sure as hell did. Two in the chest. Tell him about it Detective Delacorte." The Captain intended to make her suffer. To me, she looked as though she'd suffered enough.

"Go ahead, Detective. Fill Paxton in."

"Last five or six days, Frankie had me stop at this shop… to pick up a pack of cigarettes. I tried to dissuade him…but he always argued that as long as we had surveillance on all the suspects, he was safe. Seemed logical to me."

"Did you ever suggest that he buy a carton?" Jackson asked.

"Yeah, I asked why. He had that covered, too. Said he was trying to quit…and couldn't as long as he had extra packs handy." Her voice was a low monotone. She was tired and discouraged. Jackson wouldn't back off.

"Finish the story, Detective."

"So…I pulled up in front of the store and Frankie went in. When he wasn't back it three or four minutes, I got out and went in…found him on the floor…blood pumping out of his chest…" She shuddered before continuing. "I asked him if he knew the killer and he said…he didn't…then he died. I searched the shop and found the owner in a back storeroom unconscious…tied up. I stayed with him until help showed. Since then… I've been out with the others working the streets."

"You got any question for the Detective, Paxton?"

"No sir."

"Let me ask you one," the captain said.

"Yes sir."

"Would you allow someone you were assigned to protect leave your sight while you sat on your rear and waited for him to get hit?"

I wasn't about to add a can to Delacorte's already burdened tail. "Not being in the situation, Captain, it's hard to say. Sounds like Panteras' argument had merit… you know…all the suspects…"

"Yeah, I know, Rock." His voice softened as he spoke again to Delacorte, "You look like hell, Detective. Go home and get some sleep. Call in Monday for a new assignment. Might want to get your hair done on Monday before calling in. The way you look, you'd scare the hell out of the troops."

Delacorte's eyes brightened. She straightened her back and said, "Yes sir, I'll do that. And thank you, Captain."

"Thank me for what? The reaming? Get the hell out of here before you make Paxton bawl."

* * *

Captain Jackson and I spent a good half hour discussing a range of subjects starting with Tampa Bay Devil Rays' ineptitude and the Buccaneer's potential for a decent season. After we got past the important issues, I briefed him on my visit to Lawtey Correctional and the conclusions I'd drawn after my visit with Officer Dietrich.

"So he agreed that the attack on him was a set up to gain Sampson an early release?"

"The more he thought about it, the more certain he was that he and the Parole Board had been conned big time."

"And this guy Camarata is also out on parole and in Tampa?"

"As far as Dietrich knew. I was going to check it out with the local office on Monday."

"Why not..." he glanced at his watch before continuing. "Why not yesterday?"

"I got waylaid," I said.

"Really," he said with a lascivious gleam in his eyes.

* * *

When the three detectives arrived back in the Captain's office, it was after two a.m., and they looked as though

237

they'd been wrestling a silverback gorilla. Disheveled didn't quite make it as a description. Scruffy and smelly came close. When the captain saw them, he shook his head and said, "Good Lord. Can these be Tampa's finest? Okay men, if I wanted to discuss our situation with zombies, I'd prefer going to the nearest cemetery. You guys get your butts out of here and be back at nine a.m. tomorrow."

Agosto was the only one to speak before leaving. "Where the hell were you, Rock?"

"I stopped to see a friend after I dropped the recording on your desk. Left a note, too."

"Didn't see any damned note...then again, I haven't been in my office since noon." He stared at me for a second, then said, "You'd better go home and change shirts. You got Midge's lipstick all over the front of your friggin' shirt. See you in the morning, Casanova."

I glanced down at my shirt. There was no lipstick. Looking up, I found Agosto standing in the doorway smiling. "Gotcha," he said and walked away laughing.

PART SIX

Four Down, one to go - at least one

If you prick us, do we not bleed? If you tickle us, do we not laugh? If you poison us, do we not die? And if you wrong us, do we not revenge?

Wm. Shakespeare, Merchant of Venice, Act 111 - Scene 1

40

The *Tampa Tribune* lay open on the breakfast table, and the story of Frank Panteras' murder ran under the banner: *Man Murdered While Under Police Protection.*

Azrael wasn't surprised that the usual collection of second guessers had been interviewed and had accused the TPD of misfeasance, malfeasance, ineptitude, incompetence, and just plain stupidity. Too bad. But it couldn't be helped if the task were to be completed. Like putting Rock down. Something that had to be done. Lucky he had a hard head.

The thought of Rock brought a smile to Azrael's lips. Someday there might be an opportunity to apologize. There would be time later to express regrets. Now, it was time to plan for the fifth execution. And after that? Who knows. Only death is certain. Perhaps mine. But the debt will be paid in full.

* * *

A meeting had been scheduled for 9 a.m. with Major Tankersly. I was at my desk at seven. I noticed that Agosto was in his office, so I called. "Morning, Lieutenant. It's Rock."

"Morning, partner. How ya' feeling?"

"Okay. Surprising what a clean shirt will do for a guy's morale."

"Always happy to help a fellow officer," he said and I knew he was smiling.

"I have a question for you, Lieutenant."

"Try me."

"I was going through my case files, and I couldn't find a report on the strand of hair that was found at the Donato scene."

"You didn't get the report?"

"Nope."

"Damn. I asked Sheila to copy you. Anyway, it didn't match any current suspect."

"Didn't match April or Maggie's hair sample?"

"Like I said. No match."

"Interesting. Now, could I talk to you about my trip to Lawtey?"

"Anything that isn't on the recording? I just listened to it."

"Some thoughts that weren't recorded."

"Give me until eight o'clock. Okay?"

"Okay." I hung up and continued through my file. The Good Fairy hadn't stopped in and deposited a tip or two on her way through town. Nothing made any more sense than it had yesterday or for the preceding eight months of yesterdays. It had been almost nine months since Pete Davidson had been put down. I began to think about the night he was hit. It had been different than the others. There'd been no note from Azrael prior to the killing. In fact we'd heard nothing at all from or about Azrael before the Davidson killing.

The incident had been particularly daring. More so than the three subsequent murders. Calling 911 and reporting a robbery that hadn't started --that never occurred--took guts or stupidity. Azrael didn't seem stupid. Then waiting to commit the murder until Martino and I responded to the 911 call was more like the act of a thrill seeker…not of someone seeking revenge. Then there was the weapon. Not the same one used in the other killings. Didn't that suggest a different person?

There was also the fact that Davidson had been the only one who hadn't participated in the actual rape. And he'd been the first to name Sampson as the leader of the pack. He'd been the weak link. Had made it easier to take down the others. Perhaps the motive for his death was not the rape, but a revenge hit for turning on Sampson.

One other thing struck me as odd. When Azrael called me, he knew all of the details of the hit. However, if he didn't do the Davidson murder, how did he know all of the details the next day? Had someone on the inside passed along information? Who on the inside--other than yours truly--hated the rapists enough to commit three murders and take the blame for a fourth?

This entire cerebral harangue led me to three questions that I felt lacked answers. Three questions I took to the Lieutenant. Three questions that he took to the meeting with Major Tankersly.

41

Except for Nan Delacorte and two other detectives baby sitting Josh Sampson, all the principals were there. Major Beryl Tankersly commanded the head of the long, boat-shaped table in the conference room adjacent to his office. Captain Jackson sat to his right. The Lieutenant and I, to his left. Also at the table were Dr. Milton Bosch, Medical examiner; Dr. Agnostic "Agnes" Broadhurst, head of forensics; Detectives Jim Klein and Mike Nicholson; and Sergeant Pete Francisco, who'd been in charge of coordinating transportation and patrol unit schedules.

No one seemed too comfortable for obvious reasons. As I looked at the Major's face, I was happy that Nan Delacorte wasn't there. The Major wasn't so happy about it.

"Where's Detective Delacorte?" he asked.

"I excused her last night, Major. She was in bad shape."

"Not in as bad a shape as the man she was assigned to protect. I expected her to be here, Captain."

"I thought you would, Major. But I took a chance you'd understand that…being the conscientious officer that she is…she'd be very disturbed over the incident and…"

"Disturbed? She should damn well be disturbed. I'm disturbed. The Commissioner's disturbed. And the Mayor and the City Council are disturbed. I want her here. Pronto."

Jackson's face became a black granite mask. Hard. Firm. His eyes narrow slits. His lips closed and tight. When he spoke, his words were clipped and precise. "In my judgment, Major Tankersly, Detective Delacorte had all the humiliation she could handle when I sent her home last night. If you insist in bringing her in to suffer further indignity…"

"Damnit, I do."

"Allow me to finish, sir. If you insist, you will have my badge yet today."

Tankersly's face turned from red to purple as he glanced around the table and saw no sympathy for his position. He saw something else. A rebellion in the making. Every officer at the table--including this humble intern--reached inside his jacket. Tankersly knew they weren't reaching for a Snickers bar.

"Okay. Okay, Captain. Rather seems like an extreme reaction to a simple request," he said. He tried to smile and failed miserably. "I guess we can proceed without Detective Delacorte. I assume you'll convey my feelings in the matter, Captain. I anticipate she'll be available for any follow up inquiries?"

"Of course, Major," Jackson said.

"Good. Now let's get to the nut and bolt issues. Let me start by asking if anyone here has come up with some new ideas that could advance *your* investigation? Help us get a lock on the situation? *You've* lost three people you've had in protective custody, despite having all the manpower you've requested...and thereby blowing a hole in the division's budget. I hope you've got some answers... perhaps answers that might save the last potential victim... uh...Sampson."

"I think Intern Detective Paxton has some thoughts to share...some ideas that could point us in new directions," Agosto said.

"You have the floor, Paxton."

Somewhat surprised that the Lieutenant had passed the baton to me, I looked at him and he nodded and said, "Go over the things you discussed with me before the meeting, Rock. I think you made some good points."

"Right, Lieutenant. First, I believe we have two killers. One who killed Davidson…someone whose motive doesn't have the clarity as the one behind the murders of Donato, Pulaski, and Panteras. Azrael is definitely out to kill all who participated in April Perry's rape. The motive's very clear there."

"How do you support that conclusion, Rock? The conclusion that there were two murderers?" Jackson asked.

"First, the use of different weapons. Why change weapons? The killer was very proficient with the one he or she used on Davidson. Second, in the last three crimes, the victims received threatening letters from Azrael prior to their executions. There was no such letter prior to Davidson's murder."

"So…you don't believe the person who called after Davidson's murder was Azrael. How did he or she know all the details of the Davidson shooting? Details that never hit the news?" Agosto prompted me again. He knew my answer, an answer that I was reluctant to offer. But I did.

"Uh…yes. I believe that the person who called me wasn't Davidson's murderer. I believe the caller had to be someone on the inside…someone who knew how the 911 caller disguised his or her voice and used the same technique when taking responsibility for the murder. Someone whose voice we might recognize. Someone who…"

"You saying that Azrael could be someone at this table?" Bosch exploded in response to my theory. You saying that I…or one of my people …or one of Agnes' people…or…"

"Hold it, Milton. Let Rock finish," Agosto said.

I continued. "I'm not accusing someone at this table… God forbid…or anyone in particular. I'm saying someone with a totally different motive decided to piggy-back on the Davidson killing. Decided to complete the task that someone else started…the task of taking down the remaining four rapists. And I'm saying that the knowledge of unpublished details, the ability to out-maneuver our best efforts, the knowledge and ability to acquire specialized weapons all suggest…"

"Someone with police training. Someone who could tap and use resources not available to your average Joe or Josephine, but resources available to a current or former officer or staff member," the captain said, completing my theory.

There was a substantial silence before the Major broke in. "Paxton's thinking on this seems to open up a lot of new possibilities. Are we agreed?" There was no dissent.

Tankersly nodded and continued, "Captain, please take over. I have a meeting with the Mayor at City Hall in fifteen minutes. Wouldn't want to be late, ha ha," Tankersly stood and left the room. No one stood or saluted. I thought I heard someone say "amen".

After Tankersly left, the Captain said, "I believe that if we assume that Rock's thinking--if not on the money--could be eighty per cent correct, we've got to refocus and redirect our efforts some. I'm going to dismiss this meeting and suggest that you all spend the rest of the morning jotting down your thoughts about two things. First, the possibility that there are two murderers with distinct and different motives. Second, the possibility of a professional officer's involvement…or if not an officer…a member of the staff. I'll do the same, and we'll meet again at one a.m. in the squad's conference room. We'll all contribute our ideas and then discuss possible changes in strategy. And… uh…thanks a lot for your support, if you get my drift."

"One other thing, Captain," I said.

"Yes, Rock?"

"Although Panteras didn't recognize his killer, we still can't rule out the Perry family completely…I don't believe he'd ever seen Tommy Perdue. And I believe Sampson has to be on the suspect list."

"How's that possible,? Klein asked. "Frankie sure as hell would have recognized him."

"Sampson has a prison buddy who, I believe, is in town. And he's a guy who probably wouldn't be reluctant to kill someone for a fellow ex-con."

"Name?" Mike Nicholson asked, a ball point pen poised over a spiral note pad.

"Camarata. Rafael Camarata."

42

I left headquarters after leaving copies of my notes on the four murders with the Lieutenant. In addition to excusing me from the meeting, he gave me permission to continue pursuing the agenda I'd put together prior to my Lawtey visit. I looked at my "to do" list before starting out:

✓1. *Make appointment with April.*

✓2. *Interview prison guard involved in Josh's early release.*

✓3. *Get time for Agosto's meet with Perdue from Sheila.*

Be there.

4. *Visit Marina where Josh works. Talk to Klein. Clear with Lt.*

5. *Interview girl friend. Antonia.*

6. *Check on progress. Source of SG and Sil.*

After checking off the completed items--and finding out from Klein who had been baby-sitting Sampson--I stuck my note pad into a pocket and headed for the **Bay Shore Marina, Ltd**.

* * *

"Guess you got the Lieutenant's okay?" There was a surly tone to Detective Tino Nunez's voice after I explained my reason for visiting the marina. The word had traveled fast--the word that an inexperienced young Detective Intern had blamed a fellow cop for the Azrael murders. Of course it wasn't exactly true, but true enough to arouse some latent antipathy toward a fair-haired boy who'd gotten a leg up from the brass in some minds.

I decided to meet it head on. "I guess the word's out, Detective."

His eyebrows rose, and he stuttered a response, "Uh… what…uh… word, Paxton?"

"The word that I blamed an officer for the Azrael killings."

"Yeah, I heard that."

"I won't ask you the source, but I will clarify what I said. Okay, Detective?"

"Yeah. Okay."

"In essence, I said it would take someone with police background and or training, or someone associated with the TPD with an inside connection, to make us look as bad as we've looked. I backed up my thinking with some facts, which you probably didn't hear from your source. I've never met you, and you don't know crap about me. So let's start out even. I won't believe it if someone tells me that you beat your wife, if you won't believe I'm an a-kissing suck up trying to make it the easy way."

Nunez allowed a smile to creep across his face. "I get you, Paxton. Far as I'm concerned, I'm okay with you now…okay with any man who isn't afraid to step up to the plate and take his chances against a head hunter."

I stuck out my right hand and he took it. I felt calluses on the tips on his fingers. "You play ball, Tino?" I asked.

"Four years with the Tampa Bay Yankees, Florida State League. Play semi-pro now. Love the game."

"Pitcher?"

"Made that claim…couldn't convince the pros. Wife thinks I'm the greatest…especially since I stopped beating her."

* * *

Nunez left me with the manager of the marina, a balding, tall, sun-kissed man wearing a short-sleeved white shirt. Displayed on his right forearm was the Marine Corps insignia. Most of his left arm was missing. On his collar was a small pin showing his rank. I knew his name, but I gave him his due.

"Got some time for me, Master Sergeant? Place looks busy."

"Be happy to help you detective…if I can." He had a wide grin and blue eyes that said, "I'm a nice guy, but I can cut."

"Just a few questions about Josh Sampson."

"No problem. I know he's out on probation, and he knows he's got a job as long as he behaves himself. It's a straightforward relationship."

"He hasn't given you any problems?"

"He's still working." He nodded toward a boat hanging from davits on the land side of the sea wall. Josh was painting the bottom with an anti-fouling paint. I hadn't seen him on the way in. I don't think he noticed me either.

"Good worker?"

"On time and hasn't taken any days off.."

"What are his hours?"

"Seven a.m. to five in the afternoon. Half hour for lunch and two fifteen minute breaks…one in the morning and one in the afternoon."

"Josh get any visits from friends…at lunch time or on breaks?"

"One guy…think his name is Camarata…big guy, black curly hair and a long scar on his cheek and neck. Josh has been trying to get me to hire him. We don't need anyone right now. Told him that."

"When was the last time he visited Josh?"

"At noon…two or three days ago."

"They may be breaking their paroles," I said.

"You going to report them?" The "I can cut" signal gleamed in his eyes.

"No way. I'm sure Klein and Nunez have assured you of that."

"They did…but some guys like to show their authority. Nit pick, you know. I guess that's not you."

"Nope. So that's it. Camarata's the only person, other than employees, that you've seen with Josh?"

"Well…that's not quite right."

"Not quite right?"

"Yeah, his girl friend brings him to work and picks him up some days."

"Girl friend?"

"Yeah. Antonia Marcuso. Works nights at the Village Inn on Dale Mabry. Great place to eat."

"I may look her up," I said, "well that's about it, Master Sergeant. You've been very helpful."

"Detective, I've got to correct something. I was a Lance Corporal This pin I'm wearing…I wear it in memory of a man I served with in the boonies…in Nam. Man saved my life and got killed in the process. A great man…black guy name of Russell Johnson. Should have been me…not him." Tears dimmed the bright eyes. "I loved that man," he said.

"You got my vote for being a damned good man yourself, Corporal. Semper Fi. Hope to see you again sometime. Maybe over a beer or something more esoteric."

"Maybe a chocolate shake," he said. I walked away making a mental note to establish a long-term friendship with the man.

43

It was after midnight when I entered the Village Inn. I wanted to learn something about Josh's girl friend. I had already learned one thing. The home address of one Antonia Caruso was the same as one Josh Sampson. After checking out the two waitresses on duty, I took a seat in a section tended by a slender dark-haired girl. The other waitress was blonde and bore no resemblance to any Carusos I'd ever met. A total of two. Both men. Neither a singer.

When she came to my table, I was somewhat surprised when I read her name badge. It read, "Peggy Ann."

"Darn," I said. "I thought you might be Antonia Caruso."

She giggled, "I am. Peggy Ann and I switched badges tonight. For kicks."

"Some kick," I said.

"Why were you wanting to see me?" she asked playfully.

"For kicks." I said.

"Funny man. Really, why were you looking for me?"

"Heard you were the best damned waitress in town."

"I hope that's all you heard." She kidded right back in spades.

I was surprised to find she had a sense of humor. On second thought, I realized you'd have to have one to live with Josh. She was a pretty woman, on the near edge of being beautiful. I wondered why so many good-looking women partnered with punks.

"You still haven't said..."

"Why I came looking for you?"

"Yes. If you're on the make, you sure don't rush things."

"The honest truth? I heard Josh Sampson lived with the prettiest girl in Tampa. I had doubts and wanted to check it out."

"You're a cop, aren't you?" Her expression changed from glad to sad. Without waiting for my reply, she pulled an order pad from her apron pocket and asked, "What can I get you, sir?"

"Sorry I upset you, Antonia."

"It's okay. Just give me your order, please."

"A super double cheeseburger…mayonnaise, lettuce and tomato…and a chocolate shake. Leave out the arsenic."

"Funny man," she said, and a small smile touched her lips. All was not lost.

After finishing my shake and burger and finding out that Antonia's shift ended at five a. m., I tipped large and paid my bill after leaving a scribbled--but sincere--note on the table: *Antonia - Very sorry I tried to sneak up on you the way I did. Would like to talk to you again…all cards on the table this time. Have a feeling you're not exactly happy. Maybe I can help. Rock Paxton. I'm in the book.*

* * *

I really believed I'd have to initiate a second contact with Antonia. Wrong. At eight a.m. the following morning, my phone rang, and there she was. She sounded tired. Subdued. A two hour nap after a nine hour shift will leave any normal person subdued. And she appeared very normal.

"Detective Paxton, it's Antonia. Did I wake you?"

"No. Just finished shaving. I'm surprised you're awake, though. And please call me Rock. It's a reference to my head." She didn't laugh. I could understand why. It was too true to be funny.

"I couldn't sleep…and you seemed like a nice guy. I'd like to talk to you. I need to talk to someone."

"As I said in my note, I'd appreciate a chance to meet with you again. And maybe I can help you if you're in a jam of some sort. Give me a place and time, a place where I can buy your lunch."

* * *

We met at one o'clock p.m. at a small Cuban eatery just off Martin Luther King Boulevard. I entered the place, not expecting to accomplish much--maybe add a detail or two that would help solve our case. What I learned from Antonia was both unexpected and vindicating.

44

From a booth at the rear of the restaurant, Antonia rose from her seat and waved to get my attention. I waved back and joined her after making my way through a maze of tables and chairs.

"Hey, you look good for a gal who couldn't have gotten much sleep."

"Thanks," she said, "I took a nap after I called you. I feel okay."

I looked at her head on for the first time. She was lovely. Long dark hair framing an oval face with high cheek bones, and brown, long lashed eyes. Her features worked together to create the type of beauty one sees on travel posters--posters of Latin beauties designed to attract hot to trot male travelers to romantic island paradises.

"Thanks for meeting me," she said. "I was going to call you back... tell you I changed my mind."

"Why would you do that?"

"Because I'm scared to death." Her eyes dropped, and her lips trembled. I reached across the table and took her hands in both of mine.

"Come on, kid. Remember. I'm a cop. I'll take care of you." As I said it, I thought about our track record protecting people and winced.

"I know about you," she said, "and I don't believe he's afraid of you."

"Who's not afraid of me? Josh Sampson?"

"Yes. He said he owes you big time...something that happened years ago. Said you better stay out of his way. He's mean, Rock."

"I know how mean he is. So...how did you get mixed up with him?"

"Long story."

"I've got time."

"I grew up in a foster home in Cleveland...Ohio. When I was eighteen, I left Ohio. Bought a bus ticket and came down here."

"Were you…uh…abused by your foster parents?"

"Oh no. They were nice. But they were old….didn't have much. I felt guilty when they bought me stuff they couldn't afford."

"How long ago was that?"

"That I came to Tampa?" she asked, then answered herself. "About sixteen months ago."

"You're not twenty yet?"

"I'll be twenty in three months."

"You have no family here?"

"No."

"Okay. How'd you meet Josh?"

"I started working right away. He came in the restaurant and put on a big show. Told me how beautiful I was, and brought me flowers a few times. Roses. When he asked me for a date, I was convinced he was a nice guy…actually thought I loved him. He's handsome…and he knows it."

"You went out with him and…?"

"He more or less raped me."

"More or less?"

"Used muscle. When I said no. He…well…did it any way. If I'd resisted, he'd have hurt me bad. He's very strong, you know."

"And after that?"

"When he came in and asked me for a date, I said no… turned him down twice. One night he was waiting for me in the parking lot. Showed me a knife and made me go with him to his house….damn him…told me if I didn't live with him, they'd find me floating in Tampa Bay with my throat cut. Said his friend would do it for fun."

"All this happened right after he got out of prison?"

"I didn't know he'd been in prison…and he had a job at the Marina. I guess he'd been out for a while."

I almost asked her why she hadn't gone to the police, but I knew the answer. I could almost hear him saying, "Your word against mine…and why would they believe you? A punk kid from Ohio. You go near a cop and you're dead meat."

"You couldn't have known that his record would have worked in your favor. So…now if I help…you're willing to break away from the bastard?"

"I'd like to…but my clothes are in his house…all my stuff. And he'll come looking for me. And he will kill me if he finds me."

"I think I know a place where you'll be safe. I'll take you there after we eat."

"I need to tell you one more thing, Rock."

"Okay?"

"Josh killed that Pete Davidson guy…and I helped him."

I stared at her in disbelief. "You helped him kill Davidson? What kind of help could you give?"

"Josh introduced me to him. Had me play up to him… the poor guy. I was working evenings then. Josh said he needed to teach Pete a lesson. He had me call Pete and arrange to meet him after work…you know…at the place he got shot."

"My God. You were there?"

"Oh no. All I did was call. Josh said he was just going to rough Pete up. I had no idea he planned to kill him," she paused, sighed, and then continued. "Be honest, Rock. Am I in trouble…you know…with the law?"

"I don't think so under the circumstances, Antonia. I think I'll make other arrangements for lunch. You stay here while I make a phone call."

I'd left my cell phone in the city vehicle, so I walked to the cashier's station and flashed my badge. The clerk handed me a telephone. I dialed a number I knew better than my own. The voice that answered was also familiar. "Hi, Dad. Me? I'm fine. I have a little problem that I think you could help me with. You think Mom would be willing to feed me and a friend if I came out right now? I thought she would. Be there in twenty minutes"

I returned to Antonia and said, "Come along, kid. I want you the meet the best chef on Florida's west coast."

* * *

Escorted home by Detective Nunez, Josh parked in the driveway and entered his home through the kitchen door. Expecting to be greeted by Antonia, he was surprised by her absence. He shouted several times before storming through the house looking for her. It wasn't a large house, and he ended up in the bedroom angry and confused by her absence. He returned to the kitchen, paused, and then went to the garage behind the house. Her car was gone. But something was there on the floor. The crumpled page from a spiral pad. He read the note and exploded, "Paxton. Rock Paxton. In the book. I'll put you in a grave, you bastard."

45

Josh slammed the door as he reentered the kitchen, muttering, "I'll get the bastard. Should have killed the mother a long time ago." Crossing the kitchen, he grabbed the wall phone and dialed Camarata's number. "Rafael. Yeah, it's me. I need to get away from the cop out front. In fact, I'm going to have to get out of town. Yeah, the bitch went to the cops. Never mind how I found out. I'm going out the back way. You pick me up in the alley. Okay. Ten minutes. Yeah…and bring the money we stashed."

Josh went through the house picking up things he'd need

on the road. The last thing he dropped into his backpack was the 9mm semi-automatic he'd used to kill Davidson. This he retrieved from where it was taped to the bottom of the kitchen counter behind a drawer.

After checking to make certain Nunez was in his vehicle and not making a round outside, Sampson left the house through the kitchen door. He made his way through the garage to the alley and found it blocked by a blue Malibu.

"Going somewhere, Josh." A figure rose up from behind the vehicle. A silenced weapon was pointed at Sampson's head.

"Oh my God, it's you."

"You were expecting the Easter Bunny?" Azrael waved the muzzle of the gun toward the Malibu. "Get in. You're driving."

"Why should I? You're just going to…"

The gun spit flame and a slug tore into the fleshy part of Josh's shoulder. He screamed and grabbed the shoulder.

Azrael repeated the previous order. "Get in. The next one will hurt worse. Much worse."

One hand clutching his wounded shoulder, Josh slid into the driver's seat and started the Malibu. From the passenger side, Azrael said, "Turn left at the end of the alley. I'll give you directions from there."

* * *

On the way to my parent's home, I called Agosto and told him about Antonia's confession, which laid Davidson's murder at the feet of Josh Sampson. He seemed appropriately pleased, but ordered me to report immediately and to bring Antonia with me. I coaxed a two-hour reprieve from him. Said I'd be there at three-thirty. It was one-thirty when I hung up.

When I arrived at the old homestead, a one story rambling structure finished outside with vertical cypress and field stone. The rambling part was the result of Dad's penchant for additions: a study here, a library here, a sunroom there, etceteras. The result. Rambling.

When I told Mom that Antonia was starved, she began to work her kitchen abra cadabra while I took Dad aside and explained Antonia's situation. After I finished, he asked, "Anything personal between the two of you?"

"Nothing. I only met the girl two days ago."

"No clothes, no place to live and no job?"

"No sir. That sums it up."

"Shame. She's a pretty kid."

"She certainly is."

"You think she could work around the office? Get the mail ready? Answer the phone? Do some filing?"

"She seems bright enough to do most anything once she knows what's expected."

Well…we've plenty of room…got that little apartment I added over the garage. And I've been thinking of getting another girl in the office. One I got…Mary Jane…has been overloaded. Preparing bids running prints. You know the routine. Could pay… Antonia…minimum wage and include room and board. Think she'd be happy with that?"

"Think you could give her an advance? She had to leave her clothes and other woman stuff behind."

"Mom will take care of that. She'll enjoy it. Shopping for the daughter she never had."

I looked at my burly, rough-handed father and felt a need to hug him. So I did. "I sure love you, dad. You're the best man I've ever known."

As I pulled away from him, he tugged a handkerchief from his pocket, blew his nose and said, "What's a father for if he can't help his son with a little problem now and then."

* * *

When I arrived back at the squad room, Jim Klein looked up from his desk, stared at Antonia, and gave a silent whistle. "Lieutenant's waiting for you, Rock. The captain is with him."

"Thanks Jim. Hey, thanks also for filling Nunez in on my theory about the Azrael killings."

He dropped his eyes, then looked up, "Thought he needed to know what was going around."

"Sure. You felt obliged to say something.? Do wish you'd have filled him in with more of the details. You know...I got the impression that he didn't think much of me. Since I'd never met him...his attitude was a trifle belligerent."

"Hey, Rock...I got nothing against you."

"Yeah. And I think you're a real doll, Jimbo."

After unloading on Klein, I took Antonia by the elbow and escorted her to Agosto's office.

The door was open and Agosto saw us coming. He got up from his desk and came out to meet us. "Congratulations, Rock. Looks as though you've had a profitable couple of days." He stuck out his hand and shook mine before turning to Antonia. "And you're Miss Caruso?"

"Yes sir."

"I'm Luis Agosto, Rock's boss."

"Yes sir. He talked about you."

"Say anything nice?"

"Yes sir. Said you were a very nice guy. Said I didn't need to be afraid of taking to you."

"Well, that's the truth kid. I have a daughter who's about your age. She's a beautiful young woman, too."

"Thank you, Lieutenant," Antonia said and blushed prettily.

"Before we talk to you, Antonia, we need to discuss a couple of matters with Detective Paxton. Would you mind waiting at that empty desk over there for a few minutes? I'll have Sheila bring you something to drink if you like."

"No thanks. I'll be fine." She turned away and went to the desk Agosto had indicated.

"What's up, Lieutenant?" I asked as he led me into his office. Major Tankersly and Captain Jackson were both there.

"The Major wants to review where we are on the Azrael murders. He's been getting a lot of pressure from the Chief."

"Really," I said as Agosto's phone rang ending the pending discussion.

46

Agosto picked up the phone. "Sheila, I asked you to hold my calls…Nunez? About Sampson? Okay. Put him through." The Lieutenant listened for a several minutes. "Okay, Tino. We'll get some folks out there. Thanks." Agosto dropped the phone into its cradle and looked around his office. "Looks as though our mystery killer picked up his final victim."

"Good God. Spell it out, Luis," the Captain said.

"Tino was outside and saw a vehicle enter the alley behind Sampson's house. Went back and found Rafael

Camarata at the wheel. Cuffed him and looked around. Found blood on the pavement. Confronted Camarata who said he was there to pick Sampson up. Said he didn't know anything about the blood. Tino believes him."

"Is that it?" the Captain asked.

"No. One last thing," Agosto looked at me, "There was a note tacked to the garage siding. A note that said Azrael would be contacting you by phone with information on how to reach the place where Sampson's being held. Also, warned against putting wire taps on your phone. Said I should accompany you and…this is strange…wants us to bring April along. No one else."

"When should I expect the call?" I asked.

"Didn't say," Agosto said. "But you should probably return to your apartment and wait. Pronto."

"What about Antonia? Dad has agreed to take her in. Give her a job."

"Give me the address and we'll see that she gets there after her interview."

"Should I contact April?" I said.

"I'll take care of it."

"Why would Azrael want her to be there? So she can watch Sampson's execution? That would be brutally insensitive."

"We won't know the why's and what for's for awhile yet, will we?"

* * *

An hour after I left the squad room, my telephone rang. "Rock Paxton here."

"Hello, Rock. No questions, please. You'll get all the answers you need later. I want you to take down directions to my current location. You have paper and pen?"

"Yes…but…"

"No questions, please."

I copied the directions with no difficulty. They were given at a slow, measured pace. When finished, I laid the pen down and waited.

"Do I need to repeat anything?"

"No. I have it all."

"Have you arranged to bring April?"

"Lieutenant's handling that."

"I'm looking forward to seeing you, Rock. But there's no hurry. I won't be leaving here…and neither will Sampson."

I thought I recognized the voice. "Is this…?" A dial tone was my response. No questions asked. None answered.

* * *

After the hang up, I called Agosto. He was waiting.

"That you Rock?"

"Yes sir."

"You have the directions?"

"Yes."

"Did Azrael sound rational? Or off the wall?"

"Very rational. Very cool. Very organized."

"Good. I have April. Meet me in our downtown parking lot."

"Should be there in…say fifteen minutes."

"Let's say ten."

"May I call for a chopper?"

"Wise guy," he said.

47

After picking Sampson up behind his house, Azrael had him drive twenty or so miles south of Tampa and turn left onto a secondary road off of US Highway 41. Another turn onto a paved driveway took them to a small ranch house sitting in a grove of trees a quarter mile from the access road. To the rear of the house, stood a small barn constructed of corrugated steel. Azrael directed Sampson toward the barn and had him stop in front of an overhead door.

After opening the door with the remote control, Azrael ordered Sampson to enter the building. White faced, perspiring, and trembling, the crumbling punk pleaded for his life. "Are you...yes you are. Why do I have to...die. It was a long time ago. I've changed. I've really changed... please. I'm so sorry for what happened. I was just a stupid kid."

"Don't beg, Sampson. You're pathetic. I've been watching you for several weeks. I've seen how you treat the Caruso girl. You haven't changed a damned bit. You're still a punk, a coward, and a bully."

"Please...I'll confess to killing Pete and go back to prison. Isn't that enough to satisfy you? Isn't it enough to put me away for the rest of my life?"

"No. Not quite enough for what you did. You could never pay enough for that piece of brutality. But...in the end...killing you won't be my decision. If it were, you'd be dead already."

* * *

Following Azrael's directions, April, Agosto, and I arrived at the designated destination. We entered the driveway and parked behind the blue Malibu, which was sitting in front of the barn. Agosto looked at me and asked, "Did Azrael tell you what to do after we arrived? Any instructions at all?"

"Not a whisper beyond how to get here."

"Well, let's get up and go. The door's open, and I suppose dinner's about ready." In a coordinated move, the three of us left the vehicle. Once in the open, Agosto took out his weapon. I did likewise and chambered a round. A voice from inside the barn admonished us.

"Damned cops. Always anticipating violence. Come on in. And keep your weapons on the ready if it makes you feel safe."

We entered the barn. Agosto and I first. April a step behind. Several fluorescent fixtures overhead brightened the interior, and Azrael sat on a steel drum in the center of the open central area. He held a weapon, but it wasn't pointed at anyone. Pale and subdued, Josh Sampson kneeled on the floor in front of Azrael. The right shoulder of Josh's shirt was dark red, stiff with dried blood.

I stared at Azrael and said, "I thought I recognized your voice. Why, for God's sake? Why you?"

"Why not me? Why should it be anyone but me?"

From his seat on the steel drum, Rich Martino, TPD retired, smiled and said, "You've all met Mister Punk Sampson at one time or another under varying circumstances. And I believe he knows all of you. So introductions aren't necessary. Before I tell you why you're here, I'll put this animal in his cage."

Sarge stood and grabbed Sampson by the collar and helped him to his feet. He pushed him across the floor to an eight by ten, built-in room that occupied one corner of the barn. After a final push, which sent Josh sprawling into the structure, he closed the door and slipped a heavy lock through the hasp. Completing that task, he returned to his seat.

"The first order of business will be to determine the fate of Pretty Boy Sampson. Only one of you has a vote… the one who suffered the most at his hands. Rock and Luis…for your part…I must warn you that if you attempt to interrupt these proceedings in any way, I will kill myself or you will kill me."

48

"Sarge…for God's sake…I don't know where this is going, but don't force us to do anything we don't want to do," Luis said.

"If you're sincere…if you really don't want to be a party to my demise, you must restrain yourselves. It's that simple."

"Sarge…I don't get it," I said.

"You will by the time this little get together is over… adjourned, if you will. Now…I must get back to business. April…sweetheart…it's up to you. Do you want Sampson executed? It is totally up to you…in your lovely hands."

"Please…Sergeant Martino…I hate him…but…"

"We can't allow you to kill him," Agosto said.

"You can't stop me, Lieutenant. Sampson is already in the execution chamber. A wet floor and wires connected to a timer will do the job in…" he looked at his watch, "approximately five minutes. The circuit and timer are well concealed, so don't assume you can disarm it in time to save him. Now… April…what's your wish?"

"Sarge, please…I hate him…but I won't be a party to his execution. No. If it's for me, don't do it."

"Too bad," he said. Obviously disappointed, he left his seat on the drum and opened the structure. Josh was crouched in a corner. We couldn't see what Sarge did, but we heard the rattle of keys. After disarming his death chamber, he again locked Josh in and returned to his seat.

"Now, I'm going to tell you a story. But before I do, you must promise that not one word of what I tell you will leave this place. You will understand why when I finish."

No one spoke and via a round of nodded affirmations, we reached an agreement to honor his request.

"Good," Sarge said. "First, I must take you back to the murder of Pete Davidson. As you know, that wasn't my doing, Josh confessed to me that he murdered Pete to punish him for leading the defection of his cohorts. Like most miscreants, he blames his associates for his conviction rather than blaming his own stupidity. The gun he used is in that backpack lying against the wall." Sarge pointed at the black knapsack.

"The killing of Davidson opened the door for me. Since Rock was with me when Davison was killed, I knew I'd be the last person anyone would suspect if the others were killed…for a time anyway. I really didn't believe I would get caught. I believed it would end this way."

"But your motive…why did you take on April's rape as a personal vendetta against the…"

"Yes…this is where your promise comes in. As strange as this might   seem, April's mother Maggie was my sweetheart before she met Preston." He paused, looked at April and then continued. "We were…how do they say it…intimate…lovers on many occasions…me, a twenty two year old rookie cop and a high school senior. Then Mr. Preston Perry came along…a law school student from a wealthy family…and Maggie saw a future there and broke off our relationship. I think she loved me…but I had limited financial prospects as you and Luis probably realize, Rock. You'll get a pension and a medal or two…but you won't come close to achieving Mr. Preston's stature, power, and wealth. We're the little boys in blue who protect the big boys."

"Sounds as though you resent Perry…maybe more than you should."

"Of course I resented him. Seven months after Maggie left me for Preston, I heard she had a baby. I called her... found she'd convinced Preston that you...April...were premature. I told her I'd find out the truth somehow. Threatened to confront Preston. Maggie finally admitted that I was the father and convinced me that only the baby would be the loser if I pressed the issue. She was right, of course. I kept silent for your sake sweetheart." He smiled at April.

I looked at April. She was in shock. Her face pale. Hands clenched. Then I looked at Sarge and made a quick comparison. Tall. Hair still mostly black. Dark eyes. High forehead. Firm chin. Generous mouth. "God," I said, "he's telling the truth. You're telling the truth."

"Oh, yes." Now he was staring at April. What I saw in his eyes was not insanity, but close to it. "For a while... when you were very small...Maggie would meet me. Let me hold you. That stopped right after your second birthday. You were a bright little thing. Maggie was afraid you'd say something to Preston about me...'papa Rish' is what you called me. You were taken away from me...taken to Switzerland several years later. I missed seeing you. I missed seeing my little April shower."

"And the next time you saw her was the night of the rape?" Luis asked.

"Yes," he said and reverted to second person when referring to April, "although I didn't know she was my daughter until later at the hospital. Before I got her to the hospital, I was already heartsick and angry over the sight of such a beautiful child left cold and naked in that field...bitten... bruised...bleeding...traumatized. When I did learn who she was, I knew from that moment on that someday I would have to kill the animals who hurt her... hurt my sweet daughter...so badly."

"And you began to make plans for the others when you recognized Pete Davidson's body?"

"As I said earlier. And, Rock, you gave me additional motivation, of course."

"I gave you additional motivation?"

"Yes. I was sincerely touched by your depression when you learned why she'd left Tampa...and when I saw how she treated you...well...I knew they had destroyed you and destroyed her as a woman. Horrible consequence for a couple so intelligent ...so beautiful."

April sobbed and clutched my shoulder. I took her in my arms. "It's okay, sweetheart," I said.

Martino smiled at the sight of April in my embrace. Then he stood and said, "I'll turn my prisoner over to you, Luis. Don't forget the knapsack. And my gun, too. You should know...for the record...I got it after a drug bust. I was left alone baby sitting the dealer's car while the narcs were taking the guy in. I guess that raps it up." Sarge sighed and walked to where April stood. He touched her face gently.

"And, April, don't hate me for what I've done. Take one thing from it. I've loved you as my daughter for twenty six years. And I've loved your mother for more years than that."

Sarge unlocked the execution chamber and went in. Josh came stumbling out. Pushed hard. Sarge didn't come out. Luis ran to the door and found it locked from the inside. The overhead lights suddenly dimmed. We heard a soft buzz and the crackling sound that signified Sarge's death. We were left in semi darkness. Natural light from the outside provided adequate illumination.

For several minutes--after Luis cuffed Sampson--I continued to hold April. Luis came to my side and put his arms around both of us.

April took my handkerchief and wiped her eyes. "That night when he picked me up…and carried me to the patrol car…I felt safe. I felt a closeness to him that I could never explain. Now I know why. My father. Dear God…forgive him for what he's done."

49

We all met in the squad conference room to wrap
things up: Major Beryl Tankersly; Captain Dewayne
Jackson; Lieutenant Luis Agosto; Armorer Nick Fausto;
and Detectives Klein, Delacorte, Nicholson, Nunez and
myself. It was a post mortem--pity party--on the Azrael
case; i.e., a look at why we failed to solve the case until
after everyone was dead, including executioner Rich
Martino, a.k.a. Azrael.

We were all looking at Armorer Nick Fausto, and back
at Major Tankersly who had asked the question: "Didn't

you think it strange when Martino purchased his tazer?"

"Hell, all I knew about him was that he was a straight up guy...and it wasn't like he wanted to acquire a lethal weapon. I'm not in homicide. How was I to know someone used a tazer in a murder case?"

"Did he explain why he wanted it...the tazer?"

"Said he wanted to start a weapons collection...thought it would be a good addition."

"Nicholson, why didn't you bring Nick in sooner?"

Mike Nicholson shrugged and said, "All I know is what Nick told me at lunch today. If I'd have known sooner, I'd have brought him in sooner."

"It wouldn't have been solid proof of anything, Major," Jackson said.

"No, it wouldn't have been solid proof of anything. But purchasing his tazer when he retired...instead of turning it in...might have been cause for taking a closer look at him," Tankersly said in rebuttal, adding, "Nunez and Delacorte have checked out the last address we had for him. Neighbor says he moved himself out in a rental truck six or eight months ago. Shouldn't we have been aware of that?"

"Why should we have been aware of it? He wasn't a suspect," Luis said.

The Lieutenant had heard all the second guessing he could tolerate. I could see it in his face. "Let's face it,

Major. Martino made one mistake. The tazer. That's it. Even the murder weapon was a piece he picked up at a drug bust. No way of tracing it from what we had."

"I think it's important to examine all the facts, Lieutenant. So we don't allow four people to die under our watch again. I can see this little discussion bothers you, but I feel very right about it. We must examine all the facts if we're to improve our performance."

"All the facts, Major? Okay. Fact one, a retired police officer bought a tazer. A similar device was used in a crime. We just learned of it. Fact two, we found a black hair at one crime scene. Rich had black hair. Two of our suspects had black hair. But there was no solid mitochondria match to the suspects. A similarity, but no solid match. As a footnote, I suspect that black hair is rather common in any community with a large Hispanic population. Third fact, the weapon used in three crimes...as previously noted...was untraceable in realistic terms. Finally, Rock gave us our first decent insight into the nature of our killer. Remember? Two possible perpetrators. One of them possibly a police officer. Summarizing...and I hope I'm not boring anyone..." Agosto paused and looked at the Major before continuing. "We have three facts and two insights...which proved true...but we didn't have a damned thing that pointed to anyone in particular until Rich Martino stepped from the shadows and took bows."

The Major examined his finger nails before raising his eyes and saying, "If it all boils down to a few facts and a couple of good guesses, why are we here?"

Seeing an explosion brewing between the Major and his friend and subordinate, Captain Jackson stepped in. "I think we would accomplish a lot more if we would assign a team to study our witness protection operation. That's where we failed. That's where we need to begin correcting our procedures."

Both the Major and the Lieutenant seemed relieved by Jackson's intervention. "Good thinking, Captain. I'll rely on you to get things rolling along those lines. Well... that's it, I suppose. It's hard to believe. So damned hard to believe. A former officer of the law. A multiple murderer." Tankersly looked at me and asked, "You were with him at the end, Paxton. Did he offer a reasonable motive?"

I deferred to Agosto, he shrugged and turned his head. "Nothing specific, Major," I said. "Just what we reported to the Captain. He thought the rapists got off too easily. He'd probably had his fill, and when he saw Davidson's body, he blew. " Agosto smirked approvingly, but not so Major Tankersly would notice.

After the meeting broke up, Luis and I were standing with the Captain. He smiled and said, "You two know something you're not sharing. I won't press you, but I'm curious."

"You know what killed the cat, Captain? Be glad it's over, and that you're still in charge."

PART SEVEN

Ten Years After the beginning

I have lived enough, having seen one thing, that love hath an end

Swinburne - Hymn to Proserpine

50

Ten years after the beginning: We were sitting at a window table in the lounge at Tampa Airport's International Terminal. I looked at April across the table and tried to recall how it had been ten years earlier. How it had been the day that she sat beside me for lunch on the front campus of Armwood High. Of course that was the day I fell in love forever. At least that is what I thought then. Eighteen years old, a big time hero--in my own eyes--and in love forever.

"Thanks for coming to see me off, Rock. After

everything that's happened over the last two years, I'm surprised you'd want to talk to me…ever."

I reached across the table and took her hands. "No way I could refuse an invitation from someone I've cared for… for ten years."

"Cared for? I can recall when…as recent as two years ago…you said you loved me. That you'd always love me." She smiled and lifted my hands with hers and touched them with her lips.

"I can still say that and mean it. But it's not the same as it was ten--or just two years ago. So much has happened to both of us. We're not the same individuals we were…at least I'm not. I've thought a lot about you and me. We had very little in common at the beginning…except a flare up of young love. Love that I continued because I couldn't let go. "

"I understand, Rock. We both have new horizons. I guess one's world view changes some each year they live. How could I find out that my father was not my father and not change? How could I find out that my mother was seeing my real father regularly on the sly and not change?"

"Good Lord. She told you that?"

"Oh, yes. When I confronted her, she admitted that Martino was my father and that she met him regularly right to the very end. She also admitted that she urged him on…

urged him to murder the remaining four rapists." Tears formed in April's eyes and she dropped her head.

"Don't cry, hon. It's over. Some good things have happened. Others will if you allow them to. You've begun to feel again. The tears tell me that. Sampson got life without parole. Antonia Caruso's out from under the bastard and is working for Dad…incidentally, he says she's great. And I got my shield and a commendation. My partner lost the temporary designation. He's been confirmed as the head of Homicide. You're going to London to work for your… father's office there. A whole new view. A new you…if you allow it to happen. Perhaps you'll meet someone who'll turn things completely around for you."

Like a fresh breeze, Midge came on the scene. Her blue eyes sparkling. The highlights in her curly hair flashing gold. "Hi, guys. How's it going?" She leaned over and kissed April's cheek, pecked mine, and settled down on the chair next to me.

"What's in the bag?" I said.

"I bought you some new sport shirts. Yours are so tacky." Her enthusiasm continued as she dipped into the bag and laid out several shirts for all to see.

I shook my head and smiled. "What do you think, April? Married two weeks and she's replacing my most prized possessions…things essential to my comfort zone."

"I can see her point," April said. "The one you have on is…well tacky." We all laughed, but I wasn't quite as amused as my two loves were. The one I loved and married. The one I'd loved for ten years and kissed goodbye at the Tampa Airport.

* * *

So it is. April has gone to London and has left me with good and bad memories. As I poke around in those memories, I'm convinced I've learned more about being a man from the bad than from the good. Perhaps it takes the "bad " to make a man.

I'm writing this at a small desk--Midge calls it a secretary--in a room off of our bedroom. My bride, the mighty one, says that the room will house our *babies*. My little bride, it seems, has large ambitions. Babies! I'd lived alone for almost ten years. Now, I have Midge and the prospects of what is as yet an undetermined number of rug rats. I'm not complaining. If it's a boy, we'll call him Rock. A girl, April--even if she comes in May or June.

As I write, the soft light in the small room reaches Midge's lovely face. Tears come to my eyes as I ask myself how I could I be so lucky. Her eyes open, and she smiles seductively and asks, "Are you coming to bed soon?"

ABOUT THE AUTHOR

C. B. Wiland is an Ohio native currently residing in Lakeland, Florida, with his wife Barbara. He holds a PhD from Kent State University and ended a career spanning all levels of education as an administrator at that institution.

Printed in the United States
95374LV00004B/64-81/A